Miller's View

A NOVEL

M. W. POTTS

abbott press®
A DIVISION OF WRITER'S DIGEST

Abbott Press books may be ordered through booksellers or by contacting:

Abbott Press
1663 Liberty Drive
Bloomington, IN 47403
www.abbottpress.com
Phone: 1-866-697-5310

Because of the dynamic nature of the Internet, any web addresses or links contained
in this book may have changed since publication and may no longer be valid. The views
expressed in this work are solely those of the author and do not necessarily reflect the
views of the publisher, and the publisher hereby disclaims any responsibility for them.

Any people depicted in stock imagery provided by Thinkstock are models,
and such images are being used for illustrative purposes only.
Certain stock imagery © Thinkstock.

ISBN: 978-1-4582-1588-8 (sc)
ISBN: 978-1-4582-1590-1 (hc)
ISBN: 978-1-4582-1589-5 (e)

Library of Congress Control Number: 2014907836

Printed in the United States of America.

Abbott Press rev. date: 5/27/2014

Dedication

Let me take this moment to thank my God who closed old doors so that new doors would open; for leading me to a place of peace and quiet allowing me finish this work.

A heartfelt thanks must go to my husband Charles and my girls Kandace and Caitlin. Your love, patience and understanding gave my creativity a chance to flourish. You are all so incredibly special to me, and I couldn't have done it without you.

Detective Jonathan Miller grabs his phone, rubs his eyes and tries to focus on the clock by the bed. The voice at the other end of the line makes no sense to him.

The dispatcher tries again. "A motorist has spotted a man's body in the wooded area near exit 36 off of Route 55 in Hammond. I will tell them you're on your way."

Jonathan stretches and tries to undo some of the knots the last twenty-four hours have tied in his muscles. The tips of his fingers are just a whisper away from the ceiling. He dresses in khakis, a navy-blue polo shirt—slightly stained from last night's dinner—and his comfortable Frye slip-ons. He runs his fingers through his thick, curly hair and is on the scene within twenty minutes.

He steps out of the car and looks toward the spot where the body was found. His green eyes narrow to a slit as they follow the bright yellow crime scene tape down an embankment and about fifty feet into the thick brush.

"No ID. No wallet. Nothing in his pockets," the officer on scene informs him.

Detective Miller is now thankful for Louisiana's recent dry spell. The field he is trudging through is typically four to six inches deep in water and mud. He holds the flashlight at eye level and searches the area as he nears the victim. The grass and bushes are only slightly damaged. *The body had to have been carried.* Miller visually checks the victim and notices that he is clean and well dressed. *There is no blood or anything else to tell me what happened to this man. There is nothing on this road for miles, so where did he come from and where was he going?* One set of tire tracks is discovered leaving the area, so Miller takes pictures of the marks for comparison, but there isn't a car in sight. "Just dumped here, I guess. This is not our crime scene." His thoughts escape his lips.

Where was he killed? The young detective looks around for clues and realizes he can't see his car from where he is standing. He cannot see any of the cars. If it weren't for the flashing red and blues, he would not be able to locate them.

The bushes are so thick and the sun is just now peeking over the horizon. At the time of the call, it would have still been very dark. How could someone driving by doing a minimum forty-five miles per hour—and no one does forty-five on this stretch of blacktop —— see a body from the road?

After the emergency responders lift and load the body into the ambulance, they head for the coroner's office, and Detective Miller heads to his office. As he drives, his head spins with questions;

this is going to be a long day. Headquarters is quiet this time of the morning. Only a few scattered desk lamps illuminate the files of working officers. Miller plops his fatigued body into a worn but comfortable leather swivel chair and yanks the chain that wakes up his lamp. He needs to find a name for the victim discarded on the side of the road.

Hammond only has a population of about 17,700 people in the Parrish of Tangipahoa and more than half are women. *If this guy's a local, it shouldn't take long to ID him.* Miller fingers his well-used Rolodex and calls on longtime friend Jason Harper, his contact at the local television station.

He explains the situation and finds that Harper is all too willing to help him. Deciding it would be in poor taste to show the dead man's photo on the news, Miller has a sketch artist draw a likeness of his victim. He faxes the face to Jason, who puts it into the hands of the broadcaster. It's just in time to make the early morning news.

"Breaking news. Hammond local police need your help in identifying this person. Black male. Twenty-five to thirty-five years old. Short brown hair and hazel eyes. About 6' 1" and 170 pounds. If you have any information regarding this man, please contact Detective Jonathan Miller at Police Headquarters."

It doesn't take long before the calls come in. The locals don't mind making phone calls; just don't come knocking at the front door. That's when they tend to play the "hear no, see no, and speak no evil" game. People have seen this guy all around town, and they didn't mind letting him know. Apparently, he has been hanging around some of the local diners, antique, and hardware shops over the past couple of months, asking questions about a girl. But the call Miller is holding his breath for comes days later.

"Hammond Police headquarters. Homicide division. Detective Miller speaking."

"I know that guy you're looking for," the croaky voice says.

This gets Miller's attention and he straightens up in his chair. "How do you know him?"

"He rents an apartment from me."

"Where is this apartment?"

The voice on the other end gives Miller the address. The loud click comes before he can get a name.

"Great. Now I have a face and an address. Officer Branson, you're with me on this one." Miller grabs his sport coat and heads for the Treasure Cove Apartments about ten miles away from the 55.

Officer Branson checks to make sure he has all of his gear and then double-times it to catch up to Miller. Ted Branson is even newer to the department than the fast-rising Detective Miller and he has his eyes set on a gold detective badge of his very own.

Miller, on the other hand, hit the fast track to detective right out of the academy. Being a fourth-generation family member on the force only added to his gilded position. His quick assessment of crime scenes is unmatched in the department.

At the end of the winding road, a long, two-story building holding no more than twelve small apartments stands before them. The thick vines cover most of the upper level balcony and the bushes out front are unkempt and under watered. A few worn, wicker chairs wait patiently, yearning to be used on the long verandah.

A middle-aged man—barely chest-high to Jonathan—steps out of the side door and meets them as they approach. His thick legs and pot belly are not complemented by his partially balding head and thick glasses.

"You the landlord of this building?"

"Yeah."

"What's your name?"

"Tom Bradley"

When he speaks, Miller recognizes the voice from the phone call. He catches the tell-tale rasp of a habitual smoker in his voice and stains on his fingers.

"Follow me."

The landlord leads Miller and Branson into the apartment. Much to his dismay, he discovers nothing of value. A few pieces of furniture—remnants of a flea market—scatter the one-bedroom unit. The red plaid sofa and orange chair scream "teenage girl" against the lime green shag rug on the floor. The dark brown curtains hang on just enough hooks to keep them off the floor. Nothing matches. This man would've made Martha Stewart cry.

"The man was here long enough to make his bed. He left clothes in the closet and drawers. He didn't pack his suitcase. Everything's still here, so he must have been coming back." Branson moves throughout the room, careful not to disturb the surroundings.

Miller turns to Bradley, still nervously lurking in the doorway as he watches the detective move about the apartment. "Does this guy have a name?"

"Yeah, of course. Edwards. Donald or David. No… Daniel. Yeah, that's right. Daniel Edwards."

A search of the apartment yields no clues as to Edwards' activities. No pictures of his life are found in any of the small rooms; it's as if he's just passing through. There's no sign of a struggle in the apartment. It's sparse, but clean. No dirty dishes have been left in the sink. The refrigerator is not only empty, but clean. There's not even trash in the trash can. *He didn't have coffee or breakfast here. Maybe he ate at a local diner for breakfast.*

Miller wanders into the bathroom and rifles through the cabinets and drawers for any clues. It, too, is spotless, as if the man never used it. He catches a faint whiff of bleach. It's not fresh—maybe days old—but he can smell it. He looked into the cabinets. No bleach container. "Branson! Check the kitchen cabinets for bleach." *Weird. There's toothpaste, but no toothbrush; soap, but no towel or washcloth; shaving gel, but no razor.* He carefully lifts the can and holds it up to check for any sign of fingerprints. Nothing. "What's wrong with this picture?"

Branson just shrugs in response. "It rules out DNA testing, that's for sure. I found no bleach in the kitchen."

"Hey!" Miller turns toward Tom. "When was the last time you saw Mr. Edwards?"

"Maybe two or three days ago. Could've been a week. I don't pay attention to when my tenants come and go, ya know?"

"Has anyone been in this apartment since the last time you saw Daniel Edwards?"

"Um… I don't think so."

"Do you use a cleaning service?"

"Nope."

"Have you ever seen anyone come into this place *with* Mr. Edwards?"

"Um… I don't think so."

The young officer tries not to laugh at either the dumb answer or the croaky voice.

As Miller and the officer are about to leave, he notices a pair of round, gold-rimmed glasses on the floor, just at the foot of the orange chair. The rose-tinted lenses seem a little odd for a man. Maybe they belong to someone who visited. Miller reaches for the glasses. "What does the world look like through rose-colored lenses, Mr. Edwards?" He places the glasses on his face. "Whoooooaaa! What was that?"

He snatches the glasses from his face, startling Branson and Bradley. When he slowly puts the glasses back on, the room changes before his eyes. Images of Daniel Edwards move about in front of him. He quickly takes them off again and hands them to Branson. "Here, look in these. What do you see?"

"They're in need of a good cleaning, Sir." Branson takes them off and rubs them clean with his shirt tail.

"But what do you see?"

Officer Branson puts them back on. "You and a very ugly plastic Tiffany-style lamp." He returns the glasses to Miller.

Miller cautiously puts the glasses on again, slowly trailing his glance round the room above the rim of the glasses. As his eyes move back to the lenses, he watches as a scene unfolds before him. He looks over the rims at the officer then back at the scene in the glasses. He reaches out to touch the images, but nothing is there. "How is this possible?" He hands the glasses back to the officer. "Look again. Go on and look again!"

The young man, after seeing Miller's reaction, is reluctant, but slowly puts the glasses on again. "Sir, I don't see anything unusual. What did you see?" Branson hands the glasses back.

"Never mind." He shakes his head, hoping to clear the cobwebs. "Must not have gotten enough sleep last night or not enough coffee this morning." He decides to keep his mouth shut about the glasses. He places the glasses in a plastic bag as he and Branson leave the apartment and return to headquarters. *What the hell was that?* Miller's head whirls with the images from the glasses.

The scene in the glasses showed Edwards going through his morning routine. He made coffee, shaved, brushed his teeth, and combed his hair. He was preparing to make breakfast when he stopped and looked in the direction of his front door. Edwards appeared to have had a normal morning up to the point where he looked at the door, yet everything he used that morning was clean or missing.

What kind of glasses are these? Miller holds up the plastic bag. They appear to be just glasses—small, round, gold rims, rose tint on the lenses, but nothing unusual at all. He scratches his fingers through his thick, curly hair. Curious, Miller removes the glasses from the bag again. Running his fingers over the rims and examining the lenses and ear pieces, he searches for anything out of the ordinary. They are a puzzle to solve on their own, but that will have to wait. Daniel Edwards needs his help to find a killer.

Miller's pocket vibrates as his phone quietly informs him that someone needs his attention. He reaches in and pulls it from his pocket just far enough to read the ID screen—Ted Branson. He lets him wait.

He doesn't yet have a cause of death. The initial toxicology screen shows no alcohol or illegal drugs in his system. His phone vibrates again. This time is the coroner calling. "I have finished my preliminary report. The young man has been dead for at least six days. He must have been someplace pretty darned cold to slow decomposition, but he wasn't in the elements that long. There would be more signs of animal activity on the body. If not the insects, the gators would have gotten him. His heart looks a little inflamed. If something happened, it was quite sudden. There is no scar tissue from a prolonged heart problem. His brain, liver, and lungs are normal, so natural causes are pretty unlikely. Other than that, the young man was healthy. A heart attack is one possibility, but I can't say with one-hundred percent certainty what killed this man."

With no other leads, Detective Miller turns again to the rose colored glasses in the plastic bag. He pulls them out and examines again them from earpiece to earpiece. They look like ordinary reading glasses, but they may hold more information about what happened to the man now lying in the morgue than he might ever find anywhere else. He slowly puts them on and watches as the scene comes into focus.

Edwards walks up behind a young woman. She's dressed in a lavender sundress with a subtle ruffle at the hem. Her sandals have the tiniest of a heel and she only stands about five- foot-nothing. This makes Edwards a good head and shoulder taller, so it is easy to see over her. The two are reading the menu on the outside of a small café window. It is written in French. When the young woman turns, Miller is taken aback by her beauty. She is about to walk away—either not able to read the language or simply not interested in the selections—when Daniel steps in front of her, playfully blocking her way. He engages her in conversation. She is surprised, but she responds with a smile. She examines his face and demeanor; she seems to like that he's older and very handsome.

Daniel says just the right thing and she turns around to stay and have lunch. He talks to her with a southern boy kind of charm and smile. His hazel eyes complement his fair skin, but his smile is what seems to win her over.

They pick up their lunches and take them to a small café-style table outdoors. The opaque clouds float overhead in a sea of bright blue; it's pleasant and very warm, but the striped umbrella above them provides some respite from the afternoon sun. The light breeze plays with the ruffles of the umbrella above their heads, as well as the hem of her dress.

He's captivated by the woman. She moves with the ease and grace of a dancer. Her skin is the color of milk chocolate with a glisten of honey. Her dark hair falls into a bazillion ringlets past her shoulder, and the wide, colorful, beaded headband is the only thing keeping them under control.

They seem to enjoy each other's company and conversation. Miller watches her face. Her laughter appears light, easy, and genuine. Her smile is bright yet coquettish and says she's comfortable with her life, but her eyes tell him there's another story—much more than she's saying over lunch.

Detective Miller watches the scene, but frequently keeps his focus on the young woman as the two complete their lunch and stand to leave. Edwards reaches into his pocket and pulls out a small notepad and pen, jots down something, and hands it to her. She smiles and turns to leave. He watches her go then sits down, pulls his reading glasses from his pocket, and writes what Miller assumes is a note about their encounter as the images in the glasses begin to fade.

Miller sits at his desk and takes a deep breath as he removes the glasses and thinks of how he's going to find this woman. She may be able to give some insight as to who Edwards was and why he was here, but even if the department had the high-tech facial recognition software he'd heard so much about, he wouldn't be able to use it on the glasses.

He is not going to let that stop him. He is confident he can recreate a characterization of the woman in the glasses. Perhaps he can solve one small piece to his puzzle. He reaches for his phone and calls up the headquarters' sketch artist. When he arrives, Miller describes the young woman, giving as much detail as he can remember from the glasses. The artist captures everything from the sparkle in her eyes to the warmth in her smile.

"How's this?" The artist turns the sketch pad around to Miller. She seems to leap from the page into Miller's head.

"It's very, very good."

"She's pretty. Who is she?"

"I don't know. I'm hoping your sketch will help me figure that out."

"How did you get this much detail?"

It's almost like a memory, just not my memory. "That's a long story for another time. Thanks for your help."

He turns to his computer and types in French café and gets a short list of restaurants in the downtown area. Grabbing the paper likeness and list off his desk, he and Officer Branson head to the main part of the city. He now needs to find the café where the two had lunch.

After hours of driving through the city, they spot the table and chairs outside the Le Café on Main Street. It's exactly as he saw it in the glasses; even the fluttering umbrellas are there. He can almost visualize the couple still sitting and chatting as if nothing has happened, but something has gone terribly wrong and now this man is dead. The beautiful woman might very well be the last person to have seen him alive. They get out of the car, and Miller tries to locate the owner while Branson scours the surrounding building.

The store owner tries to take the paper from him, but he grips the paper as if afraid to let her go. The man examines the face. "Well, it kinda looks like Callie St. Claire. Yeah, that could be her. She was just here about a month ago with that guy from the news this morning."

"Do you know where I can find this Callie St. Claire?"

"I'm not sure, but I think she lives with those folks in Laplace along the river's edge."

It could take a while to find her down there. The detective's mind is spinning. He's coming up with more questions than answers. *Who is this woman? Where is she and how is she connected to Edwards? Did she kill him? Is she connected to whoever did? Why? There's always a why.*

Reaching a dead end at the restaurant, Miller and Branson head to the community of homes along the banks of the Mississippi where a whole sub-culture of people live in the wooded area that runs along the river. They've created their own language—a combination of French and broken-southern-country English—and lifestyle that keeps them separated. It always amazes Miller how they're so different from the rest of the town's people just a few miles away, but the young Branson is not excited about knocking door to door to look for this girl. He's heard rumors and stories about the people there and they make him uneasy.

Miller shows the sketch of the young woman to several residents who seem particularly nervous about his presence. "Have you seen this girl?" he asks an elderly gentleman.

The man stands chest high to Miller. His eyes are bright and sparkle with a youth that is long gone from the rest of his face and body. "Naw, Suh. I neva did see her 'round here," he answers through missing front teeth. "Her a purty lil thing, though." He laughs and almost whistles through the missing teeth.

"Thanks." Miller sighs as he heads for the next little shack in the area. He gets the same answer from the next ten houses. "Naw, Suh," is the only thing he hears. The next stop is a small, tattered cottage about fifty yards into the brush.

Miller and Branson approach the small cabin. Miller carefully navigates the dilapidated stairs of the screened porch as he moves toward the front door. The wood creaks beneath his weight, and he prays with every step that he won't go straight through.

Branson steps up behind him and to the left to peer up the wooden stairs leading to the upper level. It's too dark to see anything. A woman looks through the screen door.

"Excuse me, Ma'am. Have you seen this young woman?" Miller asks the small frame of a woman as he hands her the sketch. He towers over her, so looking beyond her into the small, dark cabin isn't difficult.

The only thing Miller can make out is a light shining through the crack close to the floor of one room. There's nothing about the place that makes him want to look around. He looks the woman up and down and notices some similarities to the drawing. Her facial structures are close enough to make her a possible relative; her hair and skin are almost the same coloring as Callie. He envisions her twenty or thirty years earlier and decides she was probably a very attractive woman in her prime, but time has not been kind. The wrinkles in her face are so deep the sweat flows through them down her face.

She scans the picture in silence for what seems like a lifetime then looks up at Detective Miller with a big grin. "Her look kinda familiar, Suh, but not sure. I see her in town sometime." Her voice has a dark undercurrent to it that is contradictory to the big smile on her face.

"Do you know her name?"

"I think I hear 'em call her Callie, but she don't live 'round these parts. Why you look for her, Suh?"

"I need to ask her some questions about a case I'm working on. Do you know where she lives?"

"Naw, Suh."

"Do you live here alone?"

"Naw, Suh. It's me and my sweet girl."

"Would you mind if I show her the picture?"

"I think she sleepin'. Maybe 'nother time."

Miller notices the smile is gone and the undercurrent has dropped a fathom. He feels a chill run down his back, despite the eighty-degree temperature of the late afternoon.

"Another time. Thanks.

Detective Miller leaves with little more than he started with. He couldn't know that a piece to his puzzle sits quietly on the other side of one of those doors. He heads back to the office, no closer to finding this woman.

He decides to pull the strange glasses from the plastic bag that holds them. He's never had such an odd source to help him with a case, but he somehow needs to find another clue to this puzzle. He slowly puts the glasses on and the images begin to flow.

Daniel Edwards watches as Callie window shops across the street. He notices that her blue jeans are slightly tattered and she's in a faded black tank top, unlike the chic attire he's used to seeing her in. Her flip flops are also faded and worn. Edwards calls out her name, but apparently his voice is drowned out by the traffic noise so he makes a mad dash across the street before he loses sight of her.

He cups his hands to his mouth and calls out again. She doesn't turn his way. He calls out yet again. She still doesn't answer. He approaches, taps her on the shoulder, and speaks to her. The touch startles the young woman out of her day dreaming over the cute sky-blue handbag and she turns to face him.

Daniel Edwards is excited and animated in his conversation. The look of confusion visibly clouds her face, but Daniel doesn't seem to notice. Miller watches intently as this scene plays out in the glasses.

Daniel seems to be doing most of the talking and after the exchange goes on for a few minutes, Miller notices a change in Callie's behavior; her posture seems uneasy as she begins to shift like a cat poised to run. She looks from side to side as if searching for the best direction in which to make her exit.

The images begin to slowly fade. "No! Not yet!"

The first images from the glasses were much different. The young woman's behavior had been more relaxed and friendly. Miller didn't see Daniel do anything that would cause Callie to act so differently. *Another piece to the puzzle.* He has to find this woman. He has to find her connection to Edwards.

Miller's thoughts are interrupted by a call from a dispatch operator.

"Detective Miller, this is dispatch. The missing vehicle in the Edwards' case has been located about three miles east of the area where the victim was found."

"I'm on my way. ETA is fifteen minutes." The face of Callie St. Claire smiles up at him from his desk. He grabs his jacket and makes his way to where the car is located.

* * *

Branson watches Miller leave the building. He waits just long enough to make sure he won't wander back up the stairs. Pretending to place a note on Miller's desk he finally catches a glimpse of the sketch Miller has been carrying around. *Cora? Why is he looking for Cora?* Branson leaves the building and makes a call.

"Hello, who is this?

"It's me, Ted. Where are you?"

"I'm at the marketplace, why?"

"Detective Miller is looking for you. He already knows where your mom lives. He is connecting the two of you to Daniel Edwards."

"I don't know a Daniel Edwards."

* * *

When Miller arrives, he's directed off the road approximately 500 feet into the trees. Apparently, someone tried to hide the abandoned car with dead brush. The small two-seat sports car doesn't appear to be damaged.

Miller checks out the inside of the car and realizes the steering wheel is too close to the seat. Edwards was pretty tall so it seems very unlikely he was the last driver. Someone shorter had to have driven the car after Daniel and, strangely, the car is just like the apartment—too clean.

He scans the scene for first impressions. He doesn't see any signs of trouble. His gaze sweeps to the tires and he's able to make a visual match to the pictures he took at the original scene. He also catches sight of footprints not far away. Someone with small feet walked through the brush and grass—away from the car—for about fifty feet before stepping toward the road.

Miller takes photos of the prints. *Another vehicle was probably waiting for them.*

"The car has been checked for prints and blood. Nothing," says the officer on scene. "The VIN tracks back to Daniel Edwards, a P.I. out of Georgia.

"Well, PIs usually travel with cameras, note pads, and other such items. Where's his stuff?"

"Nothing like that was found in the car, Sir. In fact, the car appears to have been wiped down. No fingerprints, not even his. I wish my car was this clean."

"Anybody find that odd besides me?" His fingers find their way to his hair.

"Yes, Sir."

"Okay, call Eddy's tow truck and have it picked up and taken to town. Have our people go over it again with a fine tooth comb."

"Yes, Sir. Right away."

Miller turns to leave when his phone vibrates in his pocket. He looks back as the forensic team completes their sweep of the area and bags whatever they deem important for analysis. *Someone has cleaned Edwards' apartment and his car. Murderer? Accomplice?* Miller breathes deeply to steady his nerves and mentally prepare for what's ahead. Before he sits down in the car he glances at his phone. *Two missed calls?* His screen read missed calls from Ted Branson and private number.

3

Miller needs to piece together his clues from the rose-colored glasses. Nothing is making any sense and he has to find a way to fit this puzzle into a logical order. Reluctantly, he sits back as the glasses release another secret from their hiding place.

The room is dark and hazy from the cigarette smoke. Edwards is sitting at a table, but the corner is dark. Miller knows ugly things take place in dark corners—schemes are hashed out, secrets that should never come out are revealed, and the worst of human nature is unleashed. It seems this is one such instance.

There is an envelope bulging to the point the seal is coming undone. It slides across the table with the help of the second person. The hand is large—too large to be female. It's dark and severely scarred, but the figure remains in the shadows so as not to be seen by most in the place. Moments after of taking the envelope, Edwards gets up and leaves. The scarred hand picks up its drink and retreats into the shadows.

As the images fade, Miller takes notes of the new piece to his puzzle. He gives the rose-tinted informant a short reprieve then tries again. He needs to keep pushing. His little informant does not disappoint.

Miller watches as Edwards drinks iced tea at the New Orleans train station. He fingers a small key as he watches the slow, sauntering crowd. The tiny gold key catches a light and flickers with each turn. There's something engraved on the key, but it's moving too fast to determine what it is. Something catches Edwards' attention and the key stops turning long enough for Miller to see a number eight. The subject of Edwards' attention walks toward him. Her thin-strapped dress is the color of a warm summer sky and her curly hair is pulled up off her shoulders. Her gait is a little slower than the rest of the crowd, as if her flats are hurting her feet. She has no interest in the masses around her as she clutches her matching shoulder bag tight to her body— perhaps protecting it or its contents. She has no luggage of any kind. She doesn't appear to be waiting for or retrieving another passenger.

She keeps vigil as she walks, maintaining her distance from everyone around her. Edwards watches attentively, but is careful not to get caught staring. He never approaches—never speaks. As the young woman gets closer, he looks a shade of confused Detective Miller has never seen. He feels a sense of frustration welling up as the images begin to fade. He turns to look at Officer Branson.

"We're headed to New Orleans."

"Sir?"

"I need to check out something at the N.O. Train Station."

The station is bustling with activity—pick-ups, drop offs, or people waiting for their departure time. Not many people are just strolling through without a reason. Miller scouts out the crowd.

"Detective, what are we looking for here?" Confusion fills Branson's eyes.

"Something that might take a small gold key imprinted with numbers that include an eight."

"You mean like the storage lockers?"

"Where are they?"

"I believe they're on the lower level."

"Show me."

"This way."

As they head in the direction of the lockers, Miller takes in all of the faces he passes along way, hoping against hope to get a glimpse of the young woman from the glasses. They finally locate the lockers. Miller stops in his tracks and stares at the rows and rows of lockers.

"What now, Sir?"

"We need a number eight."

"Sir? Uh… just eight or eight in combination with something else like eighty-one, one-eighty-one, or eight-one-one?"

Miller's shoulders drop hard and a shadow creeps across his face. He is feeling the strain of these vague clues and he fights back the doubt that is aggressively making its way into his head. "I don't know. Maybe someone has a master key to all of these lockers."

"I'm not sure there is one. People put their money in and take the key. I will check with management." Branson could tell from Miller's expression that he should find another answer.

"You do that."

"Yes, Sir. Right away."

From his perch against the wall, Miller has a great vantage point for watching people. The face he needs isn't coming his way. After what seems like hours later, Branson and an elderly gentleman in a grey, ill-fitted uniform finally approach.

"I'm not sure how I can help you," he says to Miller.

"I'm looking for a locker used by a young man from Atlanta. The only clue I have is that the key has the number eight on it. It could have another number, but I can't see it."

"Great! So where's the key?"

"We have no idea."

"We have over 300 lockers here. It will take hours to go through them. How will you know if you have the right one, even if we go through all of them?"

"I think we have an idea of what we're looking for and we don't need to go through all of them, just the ones with an eight in the number."

"Okay."

The gentleman and Branson head off to begin the massive locker search while Miller ponders the case. *Why is nothing fitting? Callie St. Claire, where are you?* He now carries the rose-tinted glasses in his inside jacket pocket. They are the only thing pointing him in the right direction. He puts the glasses on again, but before the images become clear, Branson comes around the corner, screaming.

"Detective! I think we found it! It wasn't eight, but thirty-eight! Thank God it wasn't 208, huh?"

Detective Miller tucks the tinted glasses back into his pocket and follows the excited Branson around the corner. The elderly station worker has the locker sitting wide open and the look of total satisfaction on his face. Miller pulls a pair of rubber gloves from his pant pocket and slips them on with the ease of a surgeon. He carefully moves things around to see what's there.

"Let's bag it all and take it back to headquarters."

"This is personal property. You can't take this." The elderly man puffs out his chest and tries to look important.

"I could get a warrant for it, but the owner of this stuff was found on the side of the road four days ago. I don't think he's gonna need it anymore." Miller turns to leave.

"Oh, sorry. Then I guess it's okay."

Officer Branson empties the contents of the locker into a large brown bag and closes the door. He thanks the station worker and hustles to catch up to Miller.

Miller is excited with their find. *Finally something useful!* Once they get everything back to headquarters, Branson takes a magnifying glass to every item in the brown paper bag while Miller takes the glasses from his pocket and faces them with steely eyes. *Why am I the only one who sees the images?* He shakes his head.

What he does know is that when he puts them on, he gets another small piece to this puzzle. Once again he slips them on his nose.

As the images clear, Miller sees Daniel and Callie. Miller can see why Daniel is interested. Callie is probably one of the most beautiful women he's ever seen in New Orleans. She is dressed in a flawless butter-yellow dress that shows the tiny curves of her waistline. Her ringlets are held up the in the back with a bedazzled barrette. They are relaxed and seem to have a lot to talk about. Miller watches them walk to a table. Callie's walk is borderline runway model—easy and graceful. It's not the awkward, painful gait from the train station. They are having dinner together. The exchange appears to be open and relaxed; the laughter seems sincere. The nervous Callie he noticed outside the store front is gone and she again is enjoying his company. Miller wonders if the girl is bi-polar. Her comfort level shifts with each vision.

Miller glances at his watch. It's late. He turns to Branson. "Maybe another run through the homes along the river will turn up something tomorrow. Go home and get some rest. We'll start fresh in the morning."

He needs to go back to his apartment. He hasn't spent much time there since this case started. A hot shower and change of clothes sounds pretty good about now. Sleep sounds even better. Maybe fresh eyes will also help.

His apartment is clean and comfortable. He had help decorating the place to make it look like a reasonably intelligent single man lived here, but even he has a few family photos sprinkled about. The Sherlock Holmes series by Doyle and top crime writers like

Baldacci and Cornwell line his book shelves, feeding his passion like sweet fruit. On his coffee table rests a small photo album of all of the victims he's been able to help; it serves as a reminder of why he does what he does. It isn't a penthouse suite in Vegas, but it is one of the nicest Hammond has to offer.

He makes a 360 degree spin and makes a mental comparison to Edwards' place. Edwards must not have been there very long and it didn't seem as though he's planning on making Hammond, Louisiana his home. He made no effort to make the apartment his personal space, even for a little while.

But someone had cleaned. Someone wanted no trace of Daniel in that apartment.

Sleep isn't going to be easy. Miller's mind is racing at a fierce pace. He reaches for his rose-tinted informant then decides the morning will be soon enough for his next clue. He needs to sleep, but he also needs to find that girl. He can see her face very clearly as he stares up from his bed. The sketch of her face is incredibly accurate. He couldn't have done any better had he handed the artist a photo. Miller sinks his head into his down-filled pillow and drifts into a coma-like sleep with Callie St. Claire's image right in front of him. The image of Callie creeps from his ceiling into his dreams.

The bright morning sun through Miller's window shouts its wake-up call. Miller throws the blanket over his head, stalling the inevitable. He is clearly not ready to get up. He realizes he shared his whole night with her, but can't quite remember what happened. He shuffles to the bathroom as if his kid brother is holding onto his ankles. *Hot shower. Yeah, that will do it. Wash that kid away.* He smiles at his own silliness.

Feeling refreshed and a little lighter in his step, he dresses and heads for headquarters. He tries to decide his next step in finding this girl. He pats his jacket pocket to be sure he has not forgotten the glasses. He knows they will provide the next clue.

The phones are ringing off their hooks at headquarters when he arrives.

Another officer screams across the room. "Detective Miller, call on two."

"Detective Jonathan Miller. How can I help you?"

"Callie St. Claire doesn't live along the river. She and her mom, Ilysa, live on the west side of Hammond, close to Route 12. And detective, hold your sketch up to a mirror."

"Who is this?"

Click.

Why do people just hang up on me? West Hammond? Then why do people keep sending me to the river? And why would I hold the sketch up to a mirror?

Miller pushes back in his chair, kicks his feet up on the edge of his desk, and closes his eyes. He runs through the crazy cast of characters.

There's the nervous Tom Bradley, Callie St. Claire, Ilysa, the man with the scarred hand and, of course, Daniel Edwards. I think I need to go back to the beginning.

Miller calls dispatch. "Yeah, this is Detective Jonathan Miller. I need a copy of the 911 call for the Edwards' case."

"I can have it for you in a couple of hours."

"Thanks. Call me when you have it."

Miller and Branson spread the evidence from the train station locker on the table in front of them, wondering where to start. Branson eyes the contents with the excitement of a child at Christmas. He notices the camera bag and decides to start there. Edwards had taken pictures of the beautiful Callie St. Claire all over town. Sometimes, she was very well dressed and groomed while at others, her clothing appeared to be tattered and worn. She often walked like a model, but it seemed at other times, she just didn't care. Edwards had been watching her for over a year. He also had pictures of Tom talking to the man with scarred hand. Although his back is to the camera in the photos, Miller can see the same hand that had crept from the shadows in the bar.

While Branson sifts through the camera's contents, Miller pulls out a small notebook and begins flipping through the pages. He stops longer on one page, smiling. "Hey, Branson. Edwards was working for the man with the scarred hand. He called his client P.S. in his notes. P.S. had Edwards looking for a woman named Ilysa James and possibly a child. Edwards tracked her from Atlanta, Georgia, across Alabama and Mississippi, to Hammond, Louisiana. He finally found the so-called child, aka Callie, who is now about twenty years old. The client has been looking for several years."

Branson's eyes glaze over as he listens. *Callie, not Cora!*

He knows most of the story. He is unaware of the connection between Edwards and the hunt for Callie and Ilysa; Cora had told him almost everything. He can be sure that if he tells Miller he knows a girl who looks like the one in the picture, his career is going to be very short. He knows how that conversation will go. The time just isn't right. He decides to stay quiet, but he doesn't know how long he has before Miller puts two and two together.

Miller pulls the glasses out of his pocket. Co-workers look strangely in his direction as he mumbles to himself, speaking his observations aloud. He knows they can't possibly know what he's experiencing, but is quite content to let them think he's talking to himself. "So, what can you tell me about this woman?" he asks, just before he puts on the glasses.

The images dance in front of him as if Edwards is pointing the way to his killer.

Ilysa's belly is full of activity. She knows the time is soon and calls her sister, Elyse, to help. Elyse feels the firm abdomen, nods her head quickly, and hurries out of the house to gather the things she'll need for the birthing.

Just days later, Ilysa feels the first pain of labor. She wouldn't be in pain for long. Her babies are impatient. Within just a few hours, Ilysa screams and pushes as she delivers her first baby girl. She's born with a full head of hair and spirit to take on the world. Callie comes into the world with a full blown yell and gasping for air, as if she knows something is wrong.

Elyse cuts the cord and wraps Callie in a blanket. She looks up and over the sheet and says something to comfort and quiet her sister as she quickly hands Ilysa her beautiful baby, Callie.

Ilysa lets out another horrible scream and begins pushing once again. The second baby comes with no noise, no movement, no breath... nothing. Ilysa holds her baby tight as she cries for her second child and softly whispers a name as their faces fade away.

Detective Miller has a new clue he couldn't have anticipated. He remembers one of the faces from the glasses. He had met her in the little house near the river's edge. She also mentioned having a baby girl. *I guess I'm going back to the river.*

It doesn't take Miller long to find his way back to Elyse's cottage. "Ma'am, do you remember helping a woman give birth to twin girls about twenty years ago?"

"Yes, Suh. I help lots of women in these parts. Twins is common here, girls 'specially."

"I think one twin didn't survive. Do you remember what happened to them?"

"Them, Suh?"

"Yeah, them. As in the woman, Ilysa James, and the baby girl she gave birth to."

"No, Suh. That was a long time ago."

"If I find that you're lying to me, I'll have you arrested for interfering with this investigation."

"If I 'member sumphin, I'll tell ya."

"I *will* find them."

"Be careful 'bout what you tryin' to find in these parts, Suh." The undercurrent in her voice is even deeper than before. "Unburyin' the past sometimes wake up ugly things." The smile fades to a look that matches her voice.

Miller turns to leave with an uneasy feeling in the pit of his stomach. He has solved over thirty homicide cases in his three years as detective on the force. This case is giving a new meaning to bizarre.

His phone buzzes. It's dispatch. "Detective Miller? The recording you were waiting for is ready."

"Great. Be right there."

Miller finds the 911 call recording on his desk when he walks into his office. He pops the tape into a small player on his desk and puts on the headphones.

"*911. What's your emergency?*"

"*I'm on Route 55 just before exit 36 and I think I see a man lying in the woods.*" The voice is low, almost inaudible.

"*Is he is moving?*"

"*I don't think so.*"

"*Is he hurt?*"

"*I don't know.*"

This time, Miller catches enough of the voice to determine it's female.

"*Is there any way you could go and check to see if he needs assistance?*"

"*I've already passed the area, but you might want to hurry. This is almost feeding time for the gators.*"

"*Can you give me your name for the detective handling the case?*"

Click. The caller disconnects.

Miller replays the tape. Which female? Callie, Ilysa, or the little woman from the river? Someone wanted Edwards found. He replays the tape. Definitely a woman. Must be someone who cares. She not only calls with a location, she specifies it is a man. She obviously knows who he is, but she must also know how he died. *What else does she know?*

Miller is typically the last one to leave the office and tonight is no different. Over and over, he listens to the taped recording of the call. He is more intrigued by what he doesn't hear than what he does. There are no sounds from the car—no sounds from outside, traffic, or any other background noises. It's deathly quiet behind the voice.

Miller shuts off the tape. He pushes back and kicks his feet up onto his desk. The recording only troubles him more. *Why didn't you call when you could have possibly saved his life?* Miller needs help finding these people and pulls the glasses from his pocket. They are his connection to this case, though he doesn't know how or why. He puts them on, anticipating the next clue.

Ilysa is asleep from the exhaustion of childbirth and Callie is asleep in a small makeshift bed next to her. Elyse is alone with the silent child. She pulls something from her pocket and vigorously rubs the baby with it. Working quickly, she warms the baby with blankets. She takes a deep breath and breathes into the lifeless child's mouth. Elyse fills the lungs of the baby with her sheer desire for Cora to live. The baby jumps just a little. Elyse breathes into the baby again. The little limbs start to move just a bit more. Her little chest rises and falls as Elyse watches, and then baby Cora opens her eyes. She's breathing. Her color becomes a little less gray.

Elyse believes she may have smiled, just a little, as if to say thank you for not leaving her. She takes this as a sign and creeps out the back door, babe in arms.

Miller's eyes widen with understanding. *There are two of them! The second one survived!*

5

After twenty years, Ilysa still grieves the loss of her baby girl. She has no idea Cora has grown into a beautiful—but dark—duplicate of Callie.

Cora didn't have the attention or education her mother had provided for her sister. She grew up along the banks of the river, educated by Elyse. Elyse left school very early in life due to a complicated pregnancy of her own that had left her barren.

Cora learned a little of the dark art along the river banks. Her interest was not strong, but she dabbled in a few things. She hated hiding from the rest of her family, but Elyse would always remind her to watch for her sister or aunt. She told her that she felt, one day, Ilysa would come home.

"You have to be careful, Cora. If you're seen, we'll both be in danger," Elyse would say. What she could never tell her was *'I brought you back from the world of the dead, stole you from your mother and sister and raised you as my own'.*

At the age of twenty, Cora is finding her own way in the world. She develops her own patterns and haunts—places she doesn't think Callie will frequent. While Callie has no knowledge of her identical twin, Cora knows almost everything, but Elyse has never explained that night.

Cora and Callie look virtually identical. Their complexions are the same and the same dark ringlets fall below her shoulders. The only difference is the small scar Cora has on her left shoulder. If she put just a little effort into it, it might look like a shooting star, at least in her eyes.

Every time she looks at her reflection, she tries to imagine what it would've been like to grow up with a twin sister. As a small child, she remembers sitting for hours at a mirror, talking to her sister and pretending Callie was in the room. Elyse would walk in and catch her and scream her disapproval, but it didn't matter—her mirrored twin was her best friend.

One day… Elyse has her sister and one day, I'll have mine.

Cora takes her musing outside and decides to walk to the river's edge. The heat and humidity of Louisiana add a glisten to her clear complexion as she strolls to her favorite spot. There is a huge toppled Oak tree in a clearing. It's quiet. She can spend hours here lost in her thoughts. There is no Callie and no Elyse. She doesn't have to hide down here. She's free to be unafraid.

The folks along the river know Elyse and Cora and she knows they'll protect them like they would their own. There are others in Hammond who know about them, too. It is hard to hide such a large, dark secret in such a small area. It's bound to peek out of the cracks and crevices of its confinement.

*   *   *

Miller continues his search for the face the sketch artist so skillfully created from his vision, but he no longer needs the pencil drawing; he now knows the face by heart. Those eyes haunt him in the darkness of his lonely apartment. The clear, chocolate-colored complexion and ringlet hair are hard to forget. Now he needs to know if he is seeing Callie St. Claire or her twin, Cora.

"Detective, hold your sketch up to a mirror," the caller said.

Now I get it.

Miller is beginning to put the pieces of this puzzle together. He now knows the confused look on Edwards' face at the train station was because he thought he was watching Callie, when it was obviously Cora. She was so different. Maybe Edwards was starting to figure out that she was an entirely different girl. Maybe he had never seen *her* before. Maybe he didn't know there were two. His notes mentioned Ilysa and one child.

Edwards' client had spent fifteen years on his own, searching for a woman and child, not knowing the woman had birthed twins. That might be a secret worth killing over.

I think I may have motive! But who would kill to protect that secret? Elyse? She faces jail time for kidnapping, if Ilysa presses charges. Cora? She could've done it to protect Elyse, the only mother she's ever known, but it's hard to put Cora into the role of murderer. P.S. needed Edwards alive to find Ilysa. Ilysa? She could've done what she needed to do to protect herself and her daughter from the Edwards' client. Callie? His heart says 'definitely not'.

Maybe Edwards was getting a little too close? Too close to Callie; too close to Ilysa. *Using Callie to find the mother could've been his plan all along.*

Miller's thoughts are interrupted as he watches a young woman walking down the other side of the street. His musing has taken his brain off guard, and it takes several seconds for it register, but even from the second floor he knows. He sees the woman who has been visiting him in his dreams. The walk is awkward, but the dark ringlets that cover her head and hang down her back are unmistakable. Miller almost falls backward out of his chair as he watches her turn into a small shop.

Snatching his jacket from the back of his chair, he runs out of his office and down the two short flights of stairs startling everyone on the office floor. He makes a crazy dash, zigzagging through traffic, across the street to the storefront. He peers into the window to make sure she's still there, but sees no sign of her. Miller walks into the store, trying to look nonplussed as he wanders about. The store clerk glances up from her receipts.

"Hello sir, do ya need some help findin' somethin'"

He smiles and politely says, "No", but keeps watch to see if she will reappear. The clerk glances up and notices him looking around the store. After looking at almost every rack in the place, Miller decides he's waited long enough.

He turns to the clerk. "Which way did the young lady go?"

"Young lady, Suh? There's no one here 'cept me and you."

"I saw her come into the store and I didn't see her leave."

"I never seen her come in. Jus' you," she says with a smile.

"What's in the back room?" he asks, pointing to the curtain behind her.

"Just storage, suh" She smiles again and goes back to doing whatever she was doing. "Have a nice day, suh" she says as Miller turns toward the door.

Miller walks back to his office. *Am I hallucinating? I know I saw her walk in here.* He lets it go for now. He decides to follow up on an idea that had come to him in the middle of the night.

Daniel Edwards, P.I. out of Atlanta.

A quick check through a missing person's database turns up nothing. Someone has to know what he was up to, who he was working for, or why he was here. Miller pulls out all the stops and calls in old favors from his connections in Atlanta. He has an academy classmate that landed on the force there.

It's worth a shot.

He hits pay dirt when he locates Jeremy Hinds from the academy, currently working with the local P.D. in Atlanta. Within forty-eight hours Jeremy gets back to him with more information than he expected. He knows a guy who overheard a conversation between these two guys about a PI who was hired by this really rich guy that was set on fire by his girlfriend because he didn't want her to have his baby. The rich guy told her that if his wife ever found out about her or the baby, she'd have his nuts stuffed and mounted on the wall. She started ranting in some crazy language, tossed his drink on his hands, and followed it with the candle from the table. His hands lit up like a torch.

Jeremy goes into the archives to find the twenty-year old police report. He finds the guy's name and description and reveals that Paul St. Claire filed a police report at the Emory University Hospital. Ilysa and her unborn baby disappeared without a trace.

Sources inform Jeremy that St. Claire spent ten years on his own and most of his assets trying to find Ilysa. He searched all of Atlanta and then all of Georgia without ever breathing a word to his wife. Edwards, being much better at tracking, would pick up from where St. Claire ended. It didn't take him long before he picked up her trail and followed her to Louisiana. *'Unburying the past sometimes wake up ugly things'. Edwards must have been close enough to really spook someone.* Miller has another clue.

Miller stops by his apartment for file he's forgotten before going back to the river. He needs Elyse to answer more questions about the twins. He opens his door and finds Celia looking through his desk.

"Can I help you find something, Celia?"

"No— no, Sir. I was just dusting and—"

"You dust the inside of my drawers? That's very conscientious…"

"You're home early. Did you forget something?"

"Yes. I forgot what I came home for. Please leave my dust inside the drawers and finish what you need to do here." He does a brief visual sweep around the apartment trying to remember his purpose for coming, but his thoughts are derailed and he turns to go back out the door.

"Yes, Sir."

Miller is really annoyed that he's forgotten what he wants from the apartment, but he finds Celia's snooping even more disturbing. *What is she looking for in my apartment?* When he leaves and heads for Elyse's house he has a new determination that she will answer his questions.

The drive there is filled with the face of Callie St. Claire... or is it really Cora? Which one fills his dreams at night and his thoughts during the day? Is she a victim, predator, or uninvolved? Miller has to find her.

He also needs to find Paul to question him. He decides to call in an APB. The all-points bulletin goes out on the dispatch radio within minutes of his request. He's described as a "person of interest", but no one has seen him. *He's got to be staying somewhere.*

He calls Branson at headquarters, his voice sounding a bit more stressed than usual.

"I need you to contact every local hotel, motel, and Holiday Inn in Hammond and all outlying areas within a two-hour drive. We're looking for Paul St. Claire—white male, brown hair, brown eyes, and severely scarred hands. He's close; I can feel it. Edwards must have told him he had made contact with one and it was just a matter of time before he found the other." He disconnects the call and returns to his thoughts.

Financial reports on Paul show that he is not as wealthy as he was twenty years ago, but he still has a little money to kick around. His wife passed away five years ago, leaving him with a substantial life insurance policy, but no children. He seems to have put his business in the hands of a CEO and put his focus into finding Ilysa and the child he never knew.

He pools most of his resources and finds Edwards, P.I., through an old friend. Edwards is young, energetic, and good at what he does. He manages to follow Ilysa's breadcrumbs across two and a half states, yet he only finds Callie. Daniel's notes mention that he never sees Ilysa, as if somehow she is aware of and manages avoids him. He watches Callie. He makes notes in the little notepad in his pocket. He watches to see if Ilysa will come out of the shadows.

Daniel tracks Callie into her mom's home state of Louisiana, but somehow manages to lose her trail. He begins going shop to shop asking questions about the beautiful, young girl. His time is spent in the local diners and small shops downtown hoping to see her. He gets lucky one day and spots her just outside the African American Museum of History and again begins his surveillance from there. Edwards keeps detailed notes as he watches Callie. His research shows she'll be at the museum of African American history every Saturday afternoon by three and she'll avoid the Marketplace. She loves to just sit at the Hessville Park and read. She sits for hours. Edwards witnesses how she seems to be liked by those around her. Talking with people in the park comes easy and even the children that come with their moms smile and play without fear. Callie's smile is warm and friendly. She's beautiful and intelligent.

Callie doesn't mind people or crowded places, but she doesn't seem to like Laplace or the people there. They are a close-knit, closed-mouthed, and dark kind of people. Most are very suspicious of strangers. Callie keeps her distance. He follows her home every night biding his time, but no matter how long he waits Ilysa eludes him.

Hammond. Louisiana will be the first face-to-face encounter between Edwards and Callie. He's grown tired of waiting and uses his southern charm to move things along a little faster. Getting closer to Callie might get him the information on Ilysa's whereabouts. Daniel moves into action because Ilysa knows how to stay one step ahead and Paul is getting agitated with his slow progress. Daniel knows he has to do something to draw Ilysa out.

7

Miller stares out of his window at the shop window across the street. How is he going to find Callie? The dark ringlet hair and brilliant smile take his focus away from the frustrating case for only a moment. His phone vibrates and breaks him from his reverie. Ted Branson shows on his ID screen and he reads the text. *Paul St. Claire has finally been located in Bogalusa at the Sportsman Inn Motel.*

It's about time. Bogalusa is about an hour away. I knew he was close. He calls Branson back.

"Miller here. Have the local PD pick him up and bring him in for questioning." He hangs up the phone smiles at seeing the light at the end of the tunnel. He just needs to find Callie, Ilysa, and now Cora. *How are these people functioning in the shadows?*

* * *

The phone rings in the dusty little office of Edwards' landlord. He swats at the pile of newspapers on his desk, sending them flying

51

to the floor, while he unburies the phone. He snatches it up just before the fifth and final ring.

"Hullo." The croaky voice is unmistakable.

"You gotta get a hold of Cora. This detective is picking up where Edwards left off. They're bringing Paul in for questioning as we speak. Miller already knows there's a twin and he's going to connect Elyse to Ilysa soon enough."

"Where's he getting this stuff from? Who's he talkin' to?"

"I dunno, but he's getting too close. They have to get out of there *now*. Once Miller talks to Paul St. Claire, he'll be coming back to the river. You'd better let Celia know what's going on, too.'"

"Celia told me she got caught snoopin' 'round his place."

"I told her to be careful. He can't find out she's been workin' for you."

"I know, I know. I'll tell her to be more careful. No more snoopin' for a while and I can get a warning to Cora and Elyse, too." The call ends with a click.

Just as he hears the click on the other end, Branson turns to see Paul St. Claire being escorted into the interrogation room by two officers and Miller. They briefly make eye contact and St. Claire looks away.

*   *   *

Miller leads St. Claire down the long brightly lit hallway and through a metal door where he is seated at a table in the small, barely-furnished room. The typical gray paint does nothing to add to his mood. One officer remains outside in the hall while the other stands inside in the far corner. Miller sits at the table, unbuttons his suit jacket, and fishes through papers in a file. He tosses the sketch of Edwards onto the table in front of him.

"Do you know this guy?"

He barely looks at the photo. "No." His hands are on the table until he notices Miller looking at them. He slowly slides them back and puts them under the table.

Miller tosses a photo taken at the coroner's lab. "Maybe this one looks more familiar."

"Kinda looks like a guy I hired a few years back. He looked a little better then. What happened to him?"

"Somebody killed him and left him for gator food. Why did you hire him?"

"Lookin' for somebody. Isn't that why most people hire PIs? Lookin' for someone or something?"

"So who are you looking for and why?"

"A woman I knew many years ago ran off carrying my child."

Miller tosses the sketch of Callie on the table.

St. Claire brings his hands back onto the table. He takes the drawing and brings it closer to him. "Is that her? Is that my girl?" His voice is low and husky, as if the words are having trouble coming out. "What's her name?"

"Edwards never told you?"

"No. I haven't talked to him since I hit Louisiana."

"Her name is Callie."

"Callie. She's beautiful. Ilysa named her after my grandmother."

"Mr. St. Claire, do you know a woman named Elyse?"

"Yes, she is Ilysa's sister."

"Sister? She's been acting like she doesn't know anything about her other than she helped her deliver the babies!"

"Babies?"

"Yeah. Ilysa delivered twin girls. The second baby was stillborn, but Elyse revived her and carried her off. She must not have told Ilysa about the baby, either." Miller watches him hard for a reaction.

"Where's the second girl?"

"Probably along the river's edge with Elyse." Miller goes to the door of the interrogation room and calls out to Officer Branson. "Take a car to the Laplace and pick up Elyse and her daughter. Bring them both in."

"Yes, Sir. I'm on it."

*   *   *

Branson rushes out of the room toward his squad car and drives toward Elyse's home. Once out of sight of headquarters, he slows his speed, takes the long way around the city, and stalls for time, hoping the Tom can get through to them in time.

Eventually, Branson arrives at the small cottage. There are no sounds or lights, except the one on the front porch. The rest of the house is dark. He knocks several times and announces himself. No answer. *Great, they're gone.*

He steps inside and looks around. The place is quiet. Furniture and pictures are there, untouched. There are dishes in the sink and the pot of soup on the stove is still warm. Most of their clothes are gone, but some are scattered on the floor. *They packed quickly.* Branson makes the call to Miller.

"They appear to have left the home recently, Sir. No indication here as to where they might be headed."

"I want an APB put out on Elyse and Cora James. Check the train station and bus terminal."

"What happens to them if you find them?" asks St. Claire.

"I'll have them brought in for questioning. I need to know what happened to Edwards and why. What exactly are *you* going to do, if and when you ever catch up to Ilysa and Callie, Mr. St. Claire? It's probably too late to press charges against Ilysa, and Callie is a grown woman, not a child. From what I've heard, you didn't want the baby. Why do you want her now?"

"Where could you have possibly heard such a thing? Ilysa? After I got released from the hospital, I tried to find Ilysa to apologize. I loved her and would have done whatever I could to make it up to her. She simply vanished. I have been searching for them for years because she and Callie are all I have left in the world since my wife died." He drops his head to hide his emotions.

Miller stands, but turns back to glance at the individual seated at his table. He shakes his head and heads for the door. "Let him sit there for a moment then kick him loose," he tells the officer just outside the door.

Miller returns to his desk and stares out the window. The young woman he noticed before has returned to the store across the street. This time, Miller knows she's inside and rushes downstairs and out the door. He races blindly across the street, nearly colliding with a car whose driver doesn't see him coming. He doesn't hesitate this time, but goes in and looks around. He heads straight for the store clerk, out of breath and pumped full of adrenalin.

"I just saw a young woman come into the store and don't tell me she didn't or I'll arrest you for obstruction of a homicide investigation! Now where did she go?"

The young woman seems startled and a bit nervous. She hesitates giving an answer as she tries to figure a way out then she straightens her posture and looks eye to eye at Detective Miller. Her whole demeanor changes. Her expression is not that of the pleasant store clerk from their past encounter. She stares at Miller as if she's in a trance. "Well, Suh. You are still mistaken. There is no one here 'cept you and me and if you didn't come to shop, maybe it's best you leave now."

Miller feels that same churning in the pit of his stomach as he had when he spoke to Elyse. He leaves the store and she immediately heads for the door, locking it tight behind him. She briskly flips the CLOSED sign over and pulls a window shade down as she walks away.

He now knows he needs help handling some of these people. This is getting weirder by the minute. He looks into the storefront window just as the clerk goes behind the register. She grabs a wool shawl and disappears through the curtain. *Why would she need a shawl? Even if she's going out the back door, it's seventy-two degrees outside today.* "Just storage" is what she'd told him. He waits a few minutes, but she doesn't return.

*   *   *

The store clerk walks down a hall filled with metal shelves of her inventory and proceeds down a long, steep flight of stairs. She walks down another hall that is shorter and dimly lit. She sees her breath as she moves along. There is a large room to her left and she can see a brightly lit room in the corner to her right. Muffled voices, speaking in a language she doesn't know, can be heard. They get louder as she gets closer, but as soon as she appears in the doorway, they stop. The two turn toward her.

"That detective mus' be watchin' my shop. He sees you coming in." She says in Cora's direction. "Someone will have to get you out through the tunnel."

"Did you tell him anything?" croaks a familiar voice.

"No, nothing, but that doesn't mean he won't be back. He's nosy, just like that other one."

"Elyse and Cora will be staying with another friend along the river for now. We have several homes there we can use." Celia's voice rings out from the darkness.

"How do we keep them safe without getting caught? Especially if he knows she's here." This is another voice, much deeper. The three turn to see Officer Branson walking their way. "I *will* lose my badge, if Miller finds out I'm involved in any way."

"You may lose your badge, but we're all facing jail!" Celia's voice rises.

"All right. Calm down. Everyone needs to keep their heads cool and mouths shut. He has no way to connect us to Elyse or Cora. As long as they stay out of sight for a while, we should be able to keep this under wraps," Tom tells them.

"Mom and I am so grateful you all have gotten involved to help us. I don't want to see any of you get in trouble."

"It's too late for that," Celia says, looking at Tom.

The small group of accomplices disperse through the tunnel and the store clerk returns to her shop.

*   *   *

Miller watches from his office window as she raises her shade, flips her door sign back to "Open" and unlocks the door. He makes eye contact with the clerk as the pool-blues smile back. It seems the pleasant clerk from before is back in the shop, but he has no idea the other four are leaving from the dark passageway beneath the store.

*   *   *

Branson appears back into the office moments later. He practically bumps into Paul St. Claire as he is leaving the building. Paul says something to Branson, but Branson doesn't respond. He just stops and watches as St. Claire walks out the door.

Miller watches the brief exchange. When Branson gets to his desk, he seems edgy and distracted.

"When you went to the home of Elyse James, what did you find?"

"Not much. It looks like they packed in a hurry. Clothes were thrown all over. Stuff in the kitchen looks like they just forgot about dinner and left. Everything else looks normal."

"I think I'll go take a look for myself."

"Suit yourself, but there is nothing there."

Miller slings his jacket over his shoulder and heads to the parking lot. The ride from Hammond to Laplace gives him time to clear his head and put his thoughts in order. *Find Ilysa.*

He picks up his cell and calls Branson. "Check the local Hammond real estate records. If Ilysa bought the home she's living in, there will be a record of sale. I don't know why I didn't think of that days ago." *Maybe I was distracted by that face.*

"I'll see what I can find." Branson begins nervously typing on his computer. He gets into the public records for real estate transactions and finds nothing under the name Ilysa James. He tries for similar names and different spellings. Of course, the only James that shows up in the computer is Elyse, but he was expecting that one. He looks for St. Claire and he is surprised to find Callie is listed as the owner of the home. He jots down the address and immediately calls Detective Miller.

8

Miller finds himself on the front porch of the home of Elyse and Cora James. The light is still on and the front door is open. He pushes it just a little as his phone rings.

"Miller here."

"I found it. Ilysa bought the home, but put it in Callie's name. I am sending the address to your phone."

"Great. Thanks."

Miller proceeds inside the home. It is as Branson described it. He slips into his rubber gloves and goes from room to room, sifting through all the things left behind. He remembers the night he spoke to Elyse and the room with the light shining under the door.

He heads there next. There isn't much left. He finds empty drawers and a few things left hanging in the closet. Miller spots something in the corner, on the closet floor —the small blue shoulder bag he remembers from the glasses. It wouldn't have seemed important to Branson. Miller opens it, but it's empty except for the faintest hint of a powdery white substance. Even with gloved hands he is careful not to touch it. Miller bags it to take back with him for analysis and continues to look around.

The scent of jasmine lingers in the air, but there's nothing else here of interest and nothing to tell him where they might've gone. He stops on the porch and looks around as he prepares to make the long ride back to Hammond. He doesn't see anyone around, but somehow feels as if someone is watching him.

He steps off of the porch and warily moves to his car. He retrieves his mystical informant from his pocket. He still doesn't understand how the glasses do what they do, but he's grateful for the help they've given so far. He slips the glasses onto his nose and lets the images fill his head.

Miller watches as the people flow through the French Market. It's one of the city's most popular shopping areas, sitting right along the river's edge. His eyes scan the crowd as they move about. Suddenly, the dark ringlets of hair appear and pass so close to Miller's face that he steps back to get out of the way.

The woman passes by slowly, then suddenly turns her back to him and moves toward another vendor's booth. She is casually dressed in cotton pants, cut-off top and the same flats she wore in the train station. Though Miller can't see her face, he's pretty sure he's watching Cora.

The woman doesn't purchase anything; she just wanders from place to place. She's approached by a smaller woman who stands directly in front of her. Neither face is visible to Miller until a young man joins them. After they turn to greet him, they move toward the closest exit. Now Miller can identify everyone in the small group. As the images begin to fade, Miller slaps the top of his dashboard so hard the shock shoots straight up his wrist and into his shoulder. *What the hell?*

The rose tinted informant has not disappointed Miller with its clue, but the secrets of Hammond are running deeper than he could have ever expected. Callie's whereabouts are still unknown. *Is she hiding or is she another victim?*

The ride home is difficult. The pain in his arm is minor compared to the fear that's jumped into his heart. Did someone get rid of Daniel and Callie in order to protect Elyse and Cora? Miller flips on his lights and siren and pushes his vehicle to the limit. He needs to get back to Hammond.

The lab for police headquarters is on the lowest level of the building and Miller goes straight there before heading to his office. He hands the lab tech the small handbag.

"There's a white substance inside. I need to know what it is, like yesterday."

"Yes, Sir. I'll get on it as soon as I can."

"No, you'll get on it now."

"Yes, Sir."

"Call me when you get a result." Miller turns to leave when his phone vibrates. "Miller here."

"This is Branson. Where are you?"

"Just leaving the lab. I'm on my way to the office."

When he arrives, he stops by his desk and checks his messages. One is from Paul St. Claire. *I'll call him later.* He types Ilysa's address into his GPS and leaves again.

Branson just misses Miller. He snatches up his phone. "Detective, I'm here at the office. Thought you said you were coming here."

"Change of plans. I'm heading for Ilysa's place. I'll let you know what I find." Miller is still a little disturbed by the last scene in the glasses. *Branson was at the marketplace with Cora and Celia. He never mentioned he even knew Cora. How does he know my housekeeper? What else isn't he telling me?*

He gets to the address Branson sent to his phone. The home is a medium-sized, southern-plantation styled home. It's an attractive and well-maintained place, very unlike Elyse's cottage along the river's edge. He climbs the short stairway in front and looks both ways on the long wrap-around porch before he rings the doorbell. He can hear the Westminster chimes play, then silence.

He waits a little longer before walking to the back of the home. The yard is neatly done with fragrant wisteria growing along the rear wall. A statue of Saint Francis stands tall and faces the house and there is a small wrought iron bench at the bottom of a huge Magnolia tree, inviting all to sit and relax a moment, but Miller has no time to relax.

He returns to his car and pulls out his phone. "Branson, I want round-the-clock surveillance on this house. I need to get an officer to keep an eye out and let me know if either Ilysa or Callie or anyone else is staying here. I also want Callie's sketch on the evening news tonight. Someone has to know where she is. If she's hiding, I want her found. Check hospitals and the morgue for any Jane Does matching her description."

Miller reluctantly returns to the car. The sky through his windshield is bright blue with a sprinkling of white feathery clouds. Callie's large bright eyes peer through the cloud to the right of him. The distraction almost takes him off the road, but he compensates and straightens his car just in time to avoid an introduction to the metal railing. His heart races from the near miss, but his mind is still on Callie. He doesn't want to think the unthinkable possibilities.

Headquarters is buzzing with activity when he arrives. He gets to his desk and finds another phone message from St. Claire. He hesitates, but decides to call.

"Mr. St. Claire? Yes, Sir. How are you?"

"I'm okay. Any news on my daughter?"

"No, Sir. Nothing yet. I've decided to put her face on the news tonight to see if we can get some help from the Hammond residents. Something should happen within the next twenty-four to forty-eight hours."

"This waiting is the hard part, but I guess if I can wait for five years, forty-eight hours will feel like a walk in the park."

"Yes, Sir. I hope that's all it is."

The afternoon ticks away slowly, what feels like half the day is only several hours later. Miller watches the large-screen TV through the glass window in his office. He can see the announcement about

Callie and stops breathing until it's finished. His exhale sounds more like *where are you?* As the broadcast ends, he sees Branson at his desk. He's already on the phone, but Miller is suspicious about his intentions. Because no one else is aware of his connection with the glasses, he must be careful how he makes his information known. It's been a day or so since he's called upon his rose-tinted informant.

The next few days are filled with phone calls and tips of every kind—that is, every kind except the one that leads him to Callie. His heart gets heavier each day Callie is missing. He rifles through his notes, going over and over everything. *What am I missing?* He re-reads all the messages on his desk and scours the files and pictures. He hasn't noticed the silence that has filled the office. When it finally hits him, he scans the room. Everyone is staring toward the entrance. When his long-range focus clears, the air is sucked out of his lungs and he gasps.

The woman with the ringlet hair and tanned, clear complexion is standing in the doorway. This time, her headband is twisted behind her head to control her wild curls. Her dress—the color of a Georgia peach—is above her knees and hugging her like a strait jacket and her matching shoes only take her an inch and a half off of floor. If he didn't know her age, she would look to be about sixteen years old.

She leans toward the officer closest to her and speaks. He turns and points with a smile in Miller's direction. She speaks again and glides across the floor toward Miller. All eyes follow her through the room and once she reaches Miller's door, they return to their business at hand.

He catches his breath, quickly stands, and closes the door to his office. When he turns around, Callie is standing just inches away.

"I've heard you're looking for me." Her voice is soft and smooth, just like her skin.

He can hear just a hint of a southern accent with a current of highly educated and proper etiquette flowing beneath it. "Yes, Ma'am. I'm glad to know you're all right." She makes him uncomfortable so he scoots around her back to his desk. "Please have a seat."

"Why wouldn't I be?" Her voice has a musical lilt to it. She sits directly in front of his chair.

"We're investigating a possible homicide, but we didn't know if you were another victim." He pulls out the sketch of Daniel Edwards and passes it across the desk.

"Do you recognize this man?"

"It looks like Daniel. Daniel Edwards. He's been following me and mom since we left Mississippi."

"When was the last time you saw Mr. Edwards?"

"A few weeks ago. Has something happened?"

"He was found dead on the side of the highway. We don't have a definite cause of death yet."

Callie's face goes blank. The lids at the bottom of her eyes become pools as they fill and overflow.

"Why would someone want to hurt Daniel?"

"We don't know yet. There are a lot of peculiar things that are going to come out. I want you to be prepared."

"Peculiar? Like what?"

"Did you know he was a private investigator?"

"He told me he his job was to find lost things."

"Yes, but did he tell you the things he was trying to find were you and your mother? Callie, have you ever met your father?"

Callie looks into Miller's eyes. The pools of tears threaten to overflow their banks again.

The look tugs at Jonathan's heart. He wants to offer a shoulder, but this was not the time or place.

"No. I just remember my mother would get very angry always tell me he didn't want me." The words catch in her throat. "We've been running from him since I was a child. My mother would tell me we were moving for other reasons, but after the fifth or sixth move, I kinda figured things out on my own."

Miller has to smile at her intuition. "He's here Callie, not far from Hammond. He wants to meet you. He sent Edwards to find you."

"I don't think my mother will like that."

"What would you like, Callie? You're grown and of age to make some choices of your own."

"I'd like to meet him. I have a lot of questions."

"I can arrange for you to meet him."

"Will you be there?"

"*Yes!* I will, if it will make you more comfortable."

"It will, thanks."

"Where are you staying?"

"I live on the west side."

"Leave your number and I'll make arrangements."

She picks up a pen and a notepad from his desk and scribbles her name and number.

Thank you, Detective."

"You're welcome. I'll be in touch."

He doesn't have the heart to throw the twin sister in on top of everything else. She obviously cares somewhat about Edwards and now he's gone. The introduction to her father will be enough for now. He'll ask about Ilysa the next time they talk. He watches her almost glide across the floor as she exits the office and his eyes stay focused on her until she disappears down the stairs. He immediately picks up the phone to call Paul.

"Hello, Mr. St. Claire. I have some good news."

"You found her?"

"Yes, actually. She came to me. I told her you were here and she has agreed to a supervised meeting."

"Supervised?"

"Yes, Sir. She's a little nervous and will meet with you as long as I'm present."

"That's fine with me. Whatever makes her comfortable. Did she happen to mention Ilysa?"

"No, Sir. We didn't discuss her yet. Maybe when we all get together you can ask her."

"Set it up and let me know. I'll be there."

The phone call ends and Miller is excited, for the moment. He still needs to connect the rest of the pieces to this puzzle to find his answer, but he'll sleep a little easier knowing Callie is unharmed.

He takes the rose-tinted glasses from his pocket and stares for a moment. *Do you know how he died?* He decides to wait until there is a little less traffic in the office before putting them on. Instead, he searches to find a suitable meeting place for father and daughter. It needs to be stylish like her, and still upscale for her dad.

La Provence. Perfect. I'll make a reservation. Miller sets things up for the following Friday night and makes both calls. Paul and Callie St. Claire are happy with the selection. He gives both the address and offers Callie a ride, but she turns him down.

"I'd prefer to meet you there."

He can hear the tremor in her voice. "Take down my number, just in case."

Back in his apartment, Miller leans back against the headboard of his bed and lets the rose-colored glasses lead him on his next adventure. *The images come into focus at the lower French Quarter in Jackson Square. It's the middle of the day and Celia, his housekeeper, is sitting on a bench. She is approached from behind by a man in a dark gray, expensively tailored suit. He stands behind her, but she never turns around. He simply puts an envelope on her shoulder. The hand holding the envelope is large, dark, and charred from burns. Miller immediately recognizes it.*

Celia takes it and he turns to leave. Miller can't tell if they exchange conversation or not. She sits a little longer and, after opening the envelope to peek inside, puts it into her purse. When she stands to leave, she hears something or someone behind her and turns suddenly toward the sound. He watches as the stumpy little man rants and raves, waving his arms about as he approaches. Miller can almost hear the croaky voice as they talk. Celia pulls the envelope from her purse and hands it to him. Tom Bradley takes the envelope and goes back the way he came. Celia continues on in the opposite direction as the images fade. The landlord from the apartment building is in cahoots with my housekeeper and Paul St. Claire? This is the second time Paul's passed a stuffed envelope to someone. He's shuffling out a lot of money for something. What could they possibly be working on together?

A chill runs down his spine. He's suddenly apprehensive about his evening with Callie and her father. He has to keep the information he's gained from the glasses his little secret, not that he could explain them anyway. He still has no idea how they work.

La Provence has the ambiance of a French inn with ceiling beams made of distressed oak. The atmosphere is warm and inviting. It's the perfect place to reunite a relationship... or even start one. The wine and food wrap guests in comfort like an old friend. Yes, this is a perfect spot.

Miller is the first to arrive. As the waiter leads him to a table set against the windows, he requests a bottle of wine be brought with water and menus. As he is being seated, he spots Paul and waves him over.

The two are only there for a few minutes before Callie appears at the entrance. Her floor-length cotton dress has a brilliant red design down the right side. Her short, red sandals are a wonderful complement to her outfit. She lets the ringlets fall where they may tonight and she looks quite breathtaking.

She makes her way to the table and Jonathan realizes that, again, he hasn't taken a breath since she walked in. This time, his sudden inhale startles him and makes him cough uncontrollably. He laughs at his own foolishness, which makes his coughing even worse. Feeling profoundly stupid and unable to stop coughing, he raises a finger at the two watching with concern and excuses himself to the men's restroom to gain control, leaving Paul and Callie alone at the table.

Paul looks at the young woman sitting across from him. "You look like your mother. Beautiful. Did you know you were named after your great-grand mother?"

"No. She never talked much about you or your side of the family."

"I guess she had her reasons."

"Her reasons? She was so hurt and angry and sometimes afraid. She thought you loved her! After the years you two had, special trips you took? After all the things you taught her? It's because of you we managed so well. Most of the money you gave her, she told me she saved it over the years. That's how she bought the house here, but she knew people would be looking for her, so she put the house in my name. If what you had then was so special, why did you tell her she couldn't have me? Look at me, Daddy. Why didn't you want me twenty years ago? Why did you send some young man to find me now? Did you know he's dead? And for what? You all of a sudden want to be daddy?"

"No, Callie. I know it's too late for that. I missed out on 'baby' Callie, but can't I get to know you from this point on? I would love to get to know the lovely young woman sitting at this table. Can't we just talk and get to know one another? I *am* your dad."

Miller returns to the table. He sees he has interrupted a serious conversation. "Again, I apologize for that... whatever that was. I hope I haven't ruined the evening. Please, order whatever you'd like." He takes a second look at Callie and looks away.

The awkward silence is broken by a delightful waitress bringing water, wine, and menus. From there, the night passes as it should. The conversation stays pretty low key and cordial.

Jonathan is pleased with evening. *This is nice... kinda like a supervised first date.*

Close to the end of the meal, Jonathan turns to Callie. "Can you tell me about Daniel? When you talked to him, what did you talk about?"

"Daniel was charming. He was funny, polite, intelligent, and attentive. We talked about everything—our childhoods, schools, siblings, everything."

"Did he ever ask you about your mother?"

Callie's eyes get wide, like a deer staring at the headlights of Miller's car. She picks up her water glass and takes a long drink. "He did," she says, almost in a whisper, "but I would always find a way to avoid answering him."

"Callie, where is your mom?"

She takes in a long, deep breath. "I don't know. I haven't talked to her in weeks. She always finds a way to get me a message to say she's all right, but I haven't heard from her for a while." The pools begin to fill at the bottom of her eyes. "We got separated in Mississippi when she was avoiding Daniel. She knew he would follow me. She always told me, if anything ever happened to her to make my way west. 'Don't stop until you get to Louisiana. I'll find you there when it's safe. There's a house there waiting for us,' she said. So that's what I did. She taught me how to travel and find safe places to sleep. She always gave me what I needed to get by. She's so smart—not just book smart, but street smart. She knew we were being followed. She showed me Daniel a long time ago. I knew who he was when he approached me at the Le Café. I acted like I didn't, but I did. But I liked him… a lot. Somehow I just knew he wouldn't hurt me." She takes in another deep breath. The exhale is slow and almost prayerful; it may have been her goodbye to Daniel.

"My mother told me to try to find my Aunt Elyse who lives near the river's edge, but I don't like going down there. I was just going to wait to see if momma was going to get here."

"We think your Aunt Elyse has left the area."

"Why would she leave? This is her home?"

"She was trying to keep Daniel from find out her secret."

"What was her secret?"

Jonathan reaches into a small briefcase and pulls out a picture of Cora. He can only tell them apart by the way they walk and dress. Cora seems a little awkward when she walks and is always more casual. Pretty, but her clothes are more worn, older, and sometimes tattered. She's still beautiful to look at and given Callie's clothes and posture, a person would need the shooting star on Cora's shoulder to tell them apart.

Miller watches her expression as Callie looks at the picture a long time. She touches the little face and her eyes fill. Her father sits quietly and watches. She looks up at Jonathan as she did in his office. "I've always felt like some part of me was somewhere else." The words struggle to come out as the tears finally leave the safety of their lids. "Do you know where my sister is, Detective Miller?" She hands the picture to her father.

"She was here in Louisiana until recently. Somewhere in Laplace. We aren't sure if she's still in the area, but I believe she is and she's usually with your Aunt Elyse. We're still looking for them."

She turns her gaze to her father. "You have gone from being childless to having twins. You didn't see that coming, did you?" She says with a little smile.

"No, Callie. I didn't. I had no idea. She's beautiful, just like you. I guess your aunt has some explaining to do to all of us."

Jonathan pushes his chair back from the table and stands. His five-foot, eleven inches looks even taller from a sitting position. "You two will have to decide what to do. In the meantime, I still have a homicide to solve. Ms. St. Claire, will you allow me to walk you to your car?"

"Yes. Thank you, Detective. You've been very helpful."

As they exit the restaurant, they pause and say their goodnights to Paul, who passes them to get to his car.

Though the night air is not cold, the temperature has dropped enough to make the air too brisk for a sundress. Jonathan smoothly slips out of his jacket and softly drapes it over her shoulders.

She simply responds with a smile. "Do you think you will find her?"

"I won't stop until I do."

He lets her slide into the driver's seat and closes her door. Through the glass, he can see the beautiful eyes staring back at him as she brushes the dark ringlets out of her face. He gently taps on the glass and motions for her to lower the window. "Maybe when this case is over you might consider having dinner with me, without the watchful eyes of dad?"

"I might consider that." She laughs lightly.

He smiles as she raises her window and drives off. Watching her drive away is the hardest thing he's had to do since this case began.

Miller takes his time on the ride home. It's lonely for the first time. He's never really found someone he wanted to include in his life, given his line of work. *Callie St. Claire could be the first possible candidate.* He smiles at the thought. *First, I have to help Mr. Edwards. He deserves an answer.*

11

He gets into the office the following morning and finds
Branson already at work. He glances out the window at
the store front across the street. The sign in the window still reads
"Closed". He'll call his apartment later to see if Celia is working at
his place today and Bradley is second on his list for people to talk
to. Somebody knows where Cora and Elyse are and they are going
to tell him.

"Branson!" he shouts, startling the young officer. "Walk with
me. Now!"

"On my way, Detective."

Miller leads him down the stairs and outside the office building.
"Let's start with how you know my housekeeper, Celia Morales."

"Huh? How did you know?"

"I know more than you think. Answer my question. How?"

"Celia and I dated in high school. We've known each other for
years."

"Why didn't you ever tell me?"

"You never asked me about Celia."

"Okay, let's get to more important matters. You never mentioned that Celia knows Tom from Edwards' apartment building. You also never mentioned that you know Cora James or that you, Celia, and Cora met at the Marketplace. Are you deliberately trying to end your career before you really get a good foothold? Because conspiracy to commit murder or accessory after the fact doesn't look good in your file when they start handing down promotions."

"I don't know where you're getting this stuff, but you've got me all wrong. Yeah, I know Celia. We're just friends. And I bumped into Cora at the Marketplace one day. I haven't known her very long and I don't know much about her."

"You'd better hope so, because if I find any evidence of you aiding Cora and Elyse or linking you to the death of Daniel Edwards, I will personally take your badge and gun and you will never see a gold shield." Miller walks away, leaving Branson dumbfounded.

Back at the office, Miller's mind drifts back to Callie, but it is short lived, interrupted by the vibration in his pocket. "Miller here."

"Yes, Sir. It's Dennis. From the lab. I have something for you."

"I'm on my way."

*   *   *

The forensic lab is bustling with science geeks of all ages. Test tubes filled with liquids of all colors are everywhere. Bunsen burners are heating up and containers are smoldering. Miller looks around at the extra little pieces to the puzzles these guys add in. *We couldn't do what we do, if they didn't do what they do.* He searches for Dennis and finds him in a corner lab.

"Whatcha got for me, Dennis?"

"I got a hit on the white substance you found in the purse. It wouldn't show up in a tox screen unless you were specifically looking for it. She probably smashed a berry in her purse. It's called *Actaea pachypoda,* also known as doll's eyes or white baneberry, the consumption of which has a sedative effect on cardiac muscle tissue and can cause cardiac arrest."

"Good job, Dennis. Thanks." Detective Miller immediately calls the coroner's office.

"Hey, Doc! I need you to pull Daniel Edwards one more time and check for a toxin called Acta... Actapakypod something. White baneberry."

"*Actaea pachypoda?* Yeah, I know the stuff. You can't eat it, and it makes a lethal wine." He laughs. "Okay. I still have a blood sample I can use. I'll let you know if I find anything."

"Thanks."

He may finally be able to connect someone to Edwards. Cora carried the same poison in her purse. He just needed to know how and when she would've been able to give it to him. She had a motive... and now means. She may have even had accomplices. *Find the opportunity and we have a slam dunk!* He still needs to find her. He needs to find Elyse.

Miller leaves the lab and heads back to his desk. Branson is at his desk, looking sheepish while talking on the phone. *Are you talking to Cora, Celia, or Elyse? You let them know I'm coming.* He stuffs his files into his briefcase and walks toward the exit.

"Detective Miller! Where are you headed? Do you need me to go with you?"

Miller stops and looks at the officer. He thinks for a moment, and then walks to Branson's desk. He leans over and gets within inches of the man's face.

"Are you working *with* me or trying to sabotage my investigation?"

"I'm with you, Sir," he whispers.

"Then let's go. I'm going to go talk to that goofy landlord again."

"Let me get my things. I'll meet you at the car."

Miller turns to leave, but as he approaches the stairs, he turns back to see Branson on the phone. *I hope I don't have to shoot that kid.* "Branson! Let's go!"

Branson says something into the phone then slams it down. He rushes to catch up to Miller. He can't be surprised by the expression on Miller's face.

The drive to the apartment building is quiet, but Miller is not in the mood for games. He goes into the rental office and finds the disheveled Tom leaning back in his chair, feet propped up on the desk and reading the newspaper.

Miller comes straight to the point. "What kind of dealings do you have with my housekeeper, Celia Morales?"

The short legs come down off of the desk and he sits up straight. He looks at Detective Miller through soda-bottle glasses, then snatches them off of his nose. They make him look like an old cartoon character. "Huh? Well, she does little odd jobs for me."

"What kind of odd jobs? And do any of them have anything to do with Cora and Elyse James or Paul St. Claire or, for that matter, Daniel Edwards?"

"Uh…"

"What do you know about the death of Daniel?"

"All I know is somebody didn't want him gettin' to close to Callie. He was startin' to spend too much time with her. She didn't want time with her to lead him back to Cora."

"Who's *she*? Elyse? How could Callie lead Edwards to Cora? She didn't know anything about Cora until recently."

"You didn't hear this from me, but Callie bumped into Elyse about four months back. They're identical, you know, and without the other one, you might not be able to tell who is who. Even Elyse was caught off guard and called her Cora by accident. When Callie told her who she was, Elyse got nervous. Elyse knew that if Callie was in town, Ilysa wasn't too far away. Elyse thought she had to hide from Ilysa, but Callie was the one mad as a snake. She figured out that she had sister that Elyse had hidden away. Don't let that pretty face fool you, Detective."

That whole scene at dinner was an act? Why'd she lie to me? "Do you know where Elyse and Cora are now?"

"Yeah. Some friends further down the river's edge are givin' them a place to stay. They didn't want to go too far."

"Take me to them. This time, no one warns them I'm coming. You lead the way and give Branson your cell phone."

The stubby little landlord hands Branson his phone and goes to his vehicle. Miller and Branson pull their squad car up behind him as he is pulling off. Driving down Route 55 and headed for Laplace, the landlord's phone buzzes. Branson reads the caller ID screen and then shows it to Miller. He shakes his head then puts his eyes back on the car that's leading him to his prime suspects. At least this time, he knows Branson isn't the one making the call.

It doesn't take them long to get the house along the river's edge. They pull up in front of a two-story house. The tall, stately columns give it the look of a southern plantation mansion, without the size.

Miller sends Branson around the back with a look that makes Branson's blood run cold. He knows the warning and proceeds around to the back door. Miller and the landlord listen at the front and they hear voices. One female and one male. Miller knocks loudly and announces himself. The sudden shuffling inside tells him he's gotten someone's attention. "Open the door. I'm looking for Elyse and Cora James."

He listens again. The shuffling gets faster and glass shatters. Miller signals Tom to stay still as Miller un-holsters his sidearm then kicks in the door to gain access. He looks around. The room is empty. He hears Branson coming in from the back door and signals him to look around the back rooms while he searches upstairs.

Going from room to room, he checks every corner until he sees a door off to his left that looks a little odd for the rest of the room. The paneling crisscrosses like the doors of a barn. All of the other doors have long, rectangular designs. He walks quietly to the door and turns the knob. *Locked!* He listens for sounds on the other side. Nothing. No footsteps. No voices. *People don't just vanish.* At that moment, Branson appears at the doorway.

"All clear downstairs," he says softly.

Miller turns his gun around and uses the handle as a hammer upon the doorknob. It doesn't take much force to knock it to the floor. Miller pushes the other end of the knob out and opens the door. They find a spiral staircase leading down into a very dark hole.

They look down the hole and back at each other. "Do you think that leads to Wonderland?" he asks as he walks past Branson and back downstairs. Miller goes to where he left Bradley and grabs him by the throat.

"Where'd they go?"

"I don't know."

"Where does the stairway lead?"

"I don't know!"

"You're part of this group who's been hiding and protecting Elyse. Where would they go next?

"I'm telling you, I don't know."

"Well, until you do know, I'm just gonna hold you for conspiracy, obstruction of an investigation, and pissing me off. Get in the squad car."

"What about my car?"

"We'll have it towed to the impound lot."

"Branson, find out who owns this house."

"Yes, sir," he says glancing briefly at the Tom.

Miller can almost feel the steam coming out of his ears. He can't believe he's this close to at least one of them and she's somehow managed to vanish into the wind. The ride back to headquarters seems to take forever. When they pull in front of the building, Miller notices the store clerk peering out the window. As they pull Tom Bradley from the backseat, she turns back to what she was doing.

Miller looks at Branson. "Find a holding room for this guy."

Branson takes the Tom inside. On the main level is a hall with eight rooms. The rooms are only connected by a large window and speakers. A large table and several chairs are the only furniture allowed. Branson shoves the Tom into one of the rooms and starts to close the door.

"You know, you not gettin' off this easy. You're just as guilty as the rest of us. When that detective finds out…." He starts to laugh as Branson slams the door closed. He leaves Tom in the room and goes upstairs to his desk. He finds Miller in his office. He's wearing the rose-tinted glasses.

"Hey, Detective. Aren't those Edwards' glasses? You like them that much?"

Miller ignores him as he carefully watches the scene in front of his eyes.

Elyse and Cora are in a field of bushes; some have the strangest looking white berry dangling from the branches. The baneberry has a small spot in the middle that, at first glance, could look like an eye. Elyse, with gloved hands, puts a bunch into Cora's small blue purse. She makes sure the clasp is tight and tells Cora something before they leave. Right now, Miller would give anything for these scenes to have sound; he never learned to read lips. The two walk across the field and get into a small motor boat waiting at the edge of the river. Facing upstream, they ride for maybe two miles and pull the silver craft out onto the opposite side. Celia is waiting for them.

Cora hands her the purse and with gloved hands, Celia removes the berries. Some are damaged, but there are enough to do the job. Elyse and Cora take off in their boat back down river. Celia takes the berries inside and begins working on them. Her back is to Miller so he doesn't see what she does, but he sees her hold up two small, capped cylinders of liquid which she then puts in her pocket and walks out the door. As the images begin to fade, Miller removes the glasses and finds Branson still standing in front of him.

"You've really taken to the rosy view, eh Miller?"

"What do you know about white baneberry?"

"I know you can't eat them… and they make a lethal wine." He laughs.

Miller doesn't see the humor in his remarks and his expression leaves no doubt. His green eyes close to a slit as Branson moves to leave, stepping backward out the door.

Miller takes off the glasses and tucks them back into his jacket pocket. He goes downstairs to the holding room where Tom is waiting, standing with his back to a large window. *He knows more than he's telling.*

"Take a seat." Miller points to one of the chairs. "What do you know about white baneberry?"

"I know you can't eat the berries…" He laughs.

"…and they make a lethal wine, yeah, I know." Miller closes his eyes and drops his head back. *Must be the standing joke of Hammond.*

"Is there anything else you can tell me about Elyse and Cora? Who else is in on hiding them?"

"I don't know everybody. That's the way people like it. That way, nobody ruins it for everybody. We take care of our own here."

"Does that include helping someone commit murder?"

"Wouldn't you do anything to protect your loved ones?"

"Not murder someone trying to do a job!"

"His job was findin' somebody who didn't want to be found by somebody else. That's not a job. That's meddlin' in somethin' that's not your concern."

"Where would they go?"

"For the last time, I don't know. They could be anywhere along the river's edge or out of Laplace completely."

Miller gets up, snatching his folder in one fell swoop, and is out the door before Tom can utter his next breath.

"But…" His word falls silent.

12

Miller gets to his leather swivel chair and plops his five-foot-eleven-inch frame down with a heavy sigh. He swings around to the window overlooking the street.

The little store clerk from across the street is staring out of the shop window. Her pool-blue eyes meet his gaze just before disappearing from the window.

Miller picks his battles and turns around to call Callie. "Are you free to meet with me?"

"I can be free around 1:30 this afternoon."

"That would be okay. Can you meet me at the cantina on West Thomas Street?"

"Yes, I know where that is. I'll be there." *Click.*

Miller arrives early and sits out in front of the store. The aroma of coffee and pastries drift past his nose. He watches the people of Hammond passing by as he waits. He wants to put the tinted lenses in place just to see what tidbit of information they hold, but decides to wait. He doesn't want to miss Callie's approach.

The sashay is unmistakable. The dark ringlets are held in order by a headband that matches the dress. The belted, button-down dress is a simple yet classy fashion statement for her; the royal blue is a nice choice and his favorite color. He opens the car door as she gets closer and stands there, one foot on the edge of the car and the other on the ground. He waits until she's next to the car to speak.

"Hello, Ms. St. Claire."

She turns toward the voice and smiles.

You are absolutely beautiful! He struggles to keep this encounter somewhat businesslike. Trying to keep his infatuation from showing on his face is getting harder for the young detective. For just a moment, Miller forgets she's here to answer more of his questions. He closes the car door and joins her on the sidewalk. With a wave of his hand, he indicates to move inside.

They locate a table outdoors, away from the crowd and make their selections. "Why'd you lie to me at dinner the other night?" He comes straight to the point.

She looks at him, her demeanor calm and her voice light and unwavering.

"Why do you assume I lied? What did I lie about?"

"You acted like you didn't know Cora, asking me if I knew where she was. You seemed surprised when you saw the picture of her... like it was the first time."

"I never said I didn't know about her." Her voice is as calm as a summer breeze. "I've known about her for months, but I've never met her. I've never seen her, so the picture you showed me really was my first time. What I said was 'I've always felt like some part of me was somewhere else' and I asked you if you knew where my sister was, Detective Miller. That is not the same as not knowing. And at no time was I lying about anything."

Her slight southern accent only adds to her allure, but he still needs to be Detective Miller until he closes this case. He can't let her get as embedded under his skin as she is in his head. He can't debate her explanation so he moves on to something useful.

"You said you liked Daniel. What else can you tell me about him that will help me find who did this to him… or don't you care?"

"Honestly, Detective Miller, I don't care. Don't get me wrong, I liked Daniel. And under different circumstances, we probably could have had something good. But he and Paul were the reason I had to keep leaving my friends, my schools and my homes. They were the reason my mom couldn't sleep at night. Daniel's job was to track down and find somebody who didn't want to be found. That's called meddlin' in other's affairs. Some people take their privacy very seriously."

"Some people take kidnapping very seriously, too. And taking a child across state lines is a federal offense. Even if it is a family member, it's against the law. Your aunt is looking at a lot of prison time. I have her on conspiracy charges, but when I add kidnapping, she may not get out. I also know your sister is involved, but if she was influenced by your aunt, they may cut her some slack. You can possibly lose them both over this mess!"

Callie lowers her eyes and drinks her tea. He can tell she's wrestling with her emotions. "What do you want me to do, Detective?"

"Help me find them. That would be a great start."

"But I don't know where they are."

"Use whatever connections you have and figure out who's hiding them."

"I can ask around, but these people protect their own. I don't know if there's anything I can do."

Miller escorts Callie back to her car. He watches her until she is out of sight and returns to his office.

Branson is at his desk, phone in one hand and pencil with paper under the other. He is feverishly trying to dig his way out of his connection with this case and maintain his career.

Miller turns to his informant. With his back to the main floor of the office, he slips on the glasses. The images begin to emerge.

Edwards comes into view. Camera in hand, he leans against the waist-high wall and photographs from a small stone bridge at the park. When Miller tries to look in the same direction, he finds the images are too far away. He has little control over the glasses and can't bring the images any closer. He can barely make out the two people on the bench, but continues to watch.

Edwards is approached by someone from behind and when he turns around, Cora is standing there. She talks first and her movements are highly animated. *She's angry. She points to the couple he's taking pictures of and yells even more. She slaps Edwards across the face and walks away quickly. He tries to follow her, but she turns to say something that stops him in his tracks. Then she leaves and so do the images in the glasses.*

"Man, why didn't you come with sound?" Miller screams at the glasses as he snatches them off of his face. It would really be nice to know what these people are saying." He calls out to Branson. "Where are the photos from Edwards' camera?"

"They're all in a folder." He moves some things around on his desk. "Here. I have them here."

Miller flips through the pile of photos until he finds the ones from the park. He can see the couple he's looking for, but still needs the picture larger to see faces. He remembers the magnifier in his desk and digs through the drawer until he finds it. It enlarges the image just enough so he can make out the familiar ringlets. She's sitting with Paul St. Claire. He appears to be wearing the same dark gray suit as before. He takes the glasses from his pocket.

I thought you were showing me images related to Daniel's murder. Why would Paul St. Claire have anything to do with his death if he was the one that hired him? How is Daniel taking pictures of St. Claire and Callie together, if they just met at the restaurant? They lied about everything. Too many pieces of this puzzle are still missing.

Miller runs his fingers through his thick waves and turns toward the window. The strange little store clerk is in the window again.

He stands up to look down at her, but this time she doesn't run or look away. *What's wrong with you?* Miller decides to go to the shop to talk face to face.

She's waiting at the shop door when he approaches and opens it as soon as he steps up. She just as quickly closes and locks it again. The blue eyes speak volumes as they fill with tears and overflow. She's as tiny and thin as a rail; her black hair only makes the river-blue eyes even brighter.

"You have something you want to tell me?" he asks softly.

"They say I can go to prison for helpin' Cora. She's been my friend for a long time. We grew up together 'long the river's edge. I just know she's scared and Elyse isn't really helpin'. It wasn't Cora's idea, ya know. Elyse put her up to it… sayin' she was going to go away for a long time, if Cora didn't help her, but I didn't know she meant to kill that young man. He was kinda nice. Nosey, but nice. Always askin' questions 'bout folk here. I'm the one that called 911 after they dropped him in the woods. I didn't want to see him get ate by the gators. He didn't deserve that. I tried to let you know where Callie was, too, and gave ya a hint about the twin, but you're a little slow." She snickers.

"Do you know where Cora and Elyse are now?"

"No. I do know they still in Louisiana, probably still 'long the river's edge, but I'm not sure who has them now. People takin' turns hidin' 'em."

"Do you know Paul St. Claire? What does he have to do with Daniel's death?"

"They told me Mr. St. Claire was Cora's daddy and he didn't even know she was alive. When Daniel found out there was two of them, he asked for more money, but Mr. St. Claire got madder than a snake."

Seems to run in the family. "Have you seen Ilysa James?"

"No, I don't think so. She never came back to the house they lived in. I live just a couple of houses down from them. Celia told me to keep an eye out in case she came back, but she never did. Just Callie. I was supposed to call her, if Ilysa showed up."

"Do you know who cleaned up Edwards' apartment?"

"His landlord, Celia and another man. I don't know his name. He helped get the body out of the apartment and into the woods. They also buried the car and cleaned it out. That's all. Am I still goin' to be in trouble?"

"Are you sure you don't know the other man?"

"Yes, I'm sure."

"Do you think you might recognize him again, if you saw his face?"

"Definitely."

"If you keep helping me like this, I'll ask the judge for leniency. You call me when and if you get anything new on any of them. You may end up on probation for a year or two."

"That's better than prison. Thank you, Detective." She wipes her face dry and walks Miller to the front door.

Miller walks slowly back to his office, trying to process everything the little clerk told him. He's almost to the front door when Branson comes bolting out.

"I found Elyse! I know where she is!"

They sprint to their vehicle and speed off in the direction of the river's edge.

"Where are we headed?"

"She went home!"

"Why would she go back there if she knows we are still looking for her?"

"Guess she thought we wouldn't go back there since we already searched it. I don't know. Maybe she thought we were busy searching everywhere else."

"How do you know she's still there?"

"Someone saw her go into the house."

"Is Cora with her?"

"They didn't mention Cora."

Miller and Branson turn on lights and siren and push their squad car to the limit. The dust from the unpaved driveway fills the air as they screech to a halt. They arrive at the small cottage and find the door open. They announce themselves and enter the house. They find Elyse sitting at her kitchen table.

Elyse watches as the men move about, a mug of teas in hand. She sips her tea as she continues to watch the men approach. She doesn't seem distressed by their presence. In fact, she seems a little too calm.

"Where's Cora?"

"She not here. Don't know where my baby girl is. You jus' remember she didn't do nothin' to that boy. I did what I had to do to protect my baby, ya know? I couldn't let them take her away from me. Not after everythin' that happened. She was just a tiny, lifeless thing, but she came back for me. It made up for all that man took away from me so many years ago. I tried to tell Ilysa, but she madder than a snake." Her voice drops low as she continues to sip her tea.

"She been my whole world for almost twenty-one years, but she grown now. I taught her how to take care of herself, my beautiful girl." Her eyes fill with tears. "She be all right without me now. She got her beautiful twin sister." Elyse smiles as her voice trails off. Her breath starts coming in short spurts she and holds her chest. Miller spots the vial on the countertop not far from the teapot and recognizes it as one of the same vials Celia had the baneberry in.

"Branson! Call 911 and get an ambulance here. Now!"

"What's wrong with her?"

"Same thing that killed Edwards! Call now!"

Branson makes the call. "Detective, what did she swallow?"

"White baneberry!"

Elyse collapses to the floor.

"Hurry! She's dying!"

"They say you can't breathe for her without getting the poison in your mouth! Just work the chest compressions. It might help a little. Help is coming."

Elyse's glazed-over eyes are more than Miller wants to deal with. "Elyse, where's Cora?"

Elyse slips quietly away. Her eyes close and her breathing stops.

Miller stops pumping her chest and sits on his knees, staring as the EMTs come to his side to check the body. They try oxygen and compressions for a few more minutes, but pronounce her dead at the scene.

Miller tells them to bag the bottle on the counter for the lab. "Branson, do you have any idea where Cora might be?"

"I know a place I can try. She used to go there sometimes when she was sad. It's down along the river."

"Show me."

They watch the EMTs load Elyse's body into the ambulance before Branson leads the way to the river's edge. They walk a good half mile along the river's bank before they see a teary-eyed Cora sitting alone on a fallen Oak tree trunk.

Miller moves slowly so as not to frighten her. She's a fragile, less confident version of Callie. He sits next to her and waits.

"My momma?" she asks through tears still caught in her throat.

"She's gone, Cora. I'm so sorry." Cora leans her head over just a little until it settles on Miller's shoulder and cries. The scent of jasmine from her hair and skin float up to Miller's nose. He sits there and lets her cry as Branson looks on from a distance. The sunshine bounces within her dark ringlets as she cries.

"What am I supposed to do now?" she asks when she finally catches her breath.

"First thing you have to do is remember everything your momma taught you. Then, I have someone who really wants to meet you. Come with me."

The three of them walk back to the car and head for the office. Miller makes a call along the way. When they arrive back at headquarters, Callie is there waiting. She's heard the news about Elyse and opens her arms wide to embrace her crying twin. Miller and Branson give them a little time before escorting them both to Miller's office. The girls sit quietly for a moment while Callie gently holds her sister's hand.

"Callie, have you heard from your mother yet?"

"Yes. I talked to her this morning. She's the one who told me about Elyse."

"How could she know? Elyse took her own life only ninety minutes ago. She couldn't have told you this morning. Maybe you misunderstood her?"

"No, Detective. I'm telling you the truth. She was crying when she told me. She said her sister's spirit whispered to her. A spirit can't talk to you unless it separates from the body."

"Where's your mother now?"

"I believe she's here in Hammond. She needs to be sure Paul is no longer a threat to her."

"Can you get in touch with her?"

"She'll get in touch with me when she thinks it's safe. Would it be all right if I take Cora home with me? She's really got no one else."

"For tonight, but don't leave town."

"We don't have anywhere else to go."

The young women leave Miller's office having lost a mother and aunt to suicide. Ilysa is still MIA, but Detective Miller still isn't sure why.

Miller gets a compulsion to use his informant once again; it's as if the glasses are calling. He slips them on and lets the images come to life.

Daniel Edwards is in his apartment, seemingly going through his morning routine. He makes coffee then goes into the bathroom. He showers, shaves, brushes his teeth, and combs his hair. He starts preparing his breakfast then suddenly stops and looks toward the door. He peeps through the tiny glass hole in the door and sees a familiar face.

Edwards opens the door for Celia and invites her in, ushers her to a chair, and pours two cups of coffee then goes back to the kitchen to cook breakfast. They're talking, but Miller hears no sound. Celia seizes the moment of inattention and slips the cylinder out of her pocket and pours it into his coffee. Edwards returns to the table with two plates of food and cream for the coffee. They chat over breakfast, but when Edwards tastes his coffee, he grimaces. Celia indicates hers is okay so he adds more sugar and cream and tries again. After a second sip of the bitter coffee, he pushes it aside, but he's already taken in enough. They talk for another moment or two when he stops talking mid-sentence and is now having trouble breathing.

Celia looks on, but offers no assistance. Daniel collapses onto the floor, clutching his chest. He looks to her for help, but she turns away, unable to witness the pain and agony she has just inflicted. She waits until she hears no more movement then slowly walks out the door, never looking back. When she gets to her car, she tosses the container behind a small bush and sits to make a phone call. Within minutes Tom appears with a tall, heavy set man.

Miller only gets a brief glimpse of his face. They wrap Edwards in a heavy tarp and carry him out the back. The tunnel access will make it easy to get him to the basement of the little shop.

The images blur before Miller's eyes and he removes the glasses. He turns back to face his desk and sees a fellow detective standing in the doorway.

"What?"

"What? What do you mean what? What's up with you and those glasses? The lights too bright in here or something?"

"No, they're not sunglasses. They—they help me think. Anyway, don't you have something better to do than stand around my office?"

Dismissed, the officer turns on his heel and walks out, closing the door behind him.

Miller picks up the phone. "This is Detective Miller. I need to get the cell phone records for Celia Morales spanning the last three months. Cross check them with the phone records for Tom Bradley at the Treasure Cove Apartments." Miller hangs up, only to make a second call. "Branson, are you anywhere near the Treasure Cove Apartments?"

"I'm about fifteen minutes away."

"Do you have gloves and bags with you?"

"Of course. My kit is always stocked."

"Go to the apartments. There are small bushes near the parking area. I need you to check carefully for a small plastic cylinder. Handle it very carefully."

It's not long before he has the phone records in hand. He makes one more call to the coroner's office to verify the official date and time of death, then checks the phone calls Celia made on that date. As he scans the pages looking for the number that matches Bradley's office, he sees another familiar number. *That number!* He knows that number. He pulls out his notes.

Gotcha!

* * *

The Louisiana sun is high and humidity is even higher. Branson checks behind every little bush in the parking area until he finally finds the right one. "Detective Miller, I found the cylinder you were looking for. Should I take this to the lab first?"

"Yes, and tell Dennis we need results now!"

He calls headquarters, "I want arrest warrants out for Celia Morales, Tom Bradley and Paul St. Claire."

Officers are dispatched to the residences and last known locations, respectively. Within hours, all are hand-cuffed, sitting in the back of squad cars, and on their way to headquarters.

Dispatch squawks on the squad car radio and announces, "Detective Miller, we have Celia Morales, Tom Bradley, and Paul St. Claire in custody."

Miller finally gets to make the call he's been waiting to make. His hands sweat a little as he picks up the phone. He calls Callie. "We have Celia Morales, Tom Bradley and Paul St. Claire in custody for the death of Daniel Edwards."

"Why would my father want Daniel dead? He hired Daniel to find us!"

"Paul had a couple of reasons. He didn't like the idea that Edwards was getting so close to you. He was hired to find you and your mother, not get emotionally involved with you. Once Daniel found out there were actually two of you, he upped the price, got greedy, and your dad didn't want to pay. We know your dad paid Tom Bradley and Celia for their parts, and we also confirmed your father's involvement with Celia through their cell phone records. We know she called him right after she killed Edwards. We found the container she used for the white baneberry. The lab is checking for prints and traces of the poison. Once they confirm my suspicions, we can close this case. By the way, how's Cora?"

"She's fine; sleeping now. She took Elyse's suicide really hard."

"I'm sure. I have nothing physical linking her to Daniel's death, and without Elyse's testimony there is no one to say she participated. I don't think any of the people who did so much to protect her are going to put her in harm's way now. So it looks like she's off the hook. If I hear anything else, I'll call."

"Thank you, Detective Miller."

He wishes he had something else to talk to her about, but lets her hang up. With this case coming to a close, he wonders if she will talk to him again. His cell phone vibrates in his pocket. It's Dennis.

"Detective Miller, it's Dennis. I've got good news and weird news. Which do you want first?"

"Give me the good news."

"Okay. The cylinder found outside of Daniel Edwards' apartment had enough trace in it to test. It tested positive for Actaea pachypoda, and the prints on it came back to Celia Morales. The weird news is the second cylinder found in the home of Elyse James came back positive for Actaea pachypoda also, but the prints aren't hers so you might consider ruling out suicide."

"Whose prints are they?"

"Don't know. They're not in the database."

Damn!

Also available, *As I See It: A Young Woman's Strange Obsession Confession*, the journey of a woman struggling with a type of Hypomanic Disorder and the battle to overcome her delusion. The sequel: *The Heart of A Dream* is soon to follow.